DOCTOR WHO
THE GUNFIGHTERS

For TAMSIN,
with coloured moon clouds

DOCTOR WHO
THE GUNFIGHTERS

Based on the BBC television serial by Donald Cotton by arrangement with the British Broadcasting Corporation

DONALD COTTON

Number 101
in the Doctor Who Library

A TARGET BOOK
published by
the Paperback Division of
W.H. ALLEN & Co. PLC

A Target Book
Published in 1986
By the Paperback Division of
W.H. Allen & Co. PLC
44 Hill Street, London W1X 8LB

First published in Great Britain by
W.H. Allen & Co. PLC in 1985

Printed and bound in Great Britain by
Anchor Brendon Ltd, Tiptree, Essex

The BBC producer of *The Gunfighters* was Innes Lloyd,
the director was Rex Tucker

ISBN 0 426 20195 7

CONTENTS

Prologue

The Sanatorium at Glenwood Springs, Colorado, was never a place you'd visit for your health: but, at least, the management would usually arrange for you to die there in some sort of comfort; which is better, to my way of thinking, than meeting your Maker in some gun-loud back alley, without the benefit of booze.

So, for a few dollars more, supplies of your favourite hooch could continue to rot what was left of your carcass; until the therapeutic sulphur fumes, for which the place was renowned, finally clogged your breath beyond redemption.

'Tomb Service', it was called, by the moribund inmates; for if a man can't joke at a time like that, when in hell can he? *Except* in hell, of course.

On the other hand, if your credit ran out before your lungs caved in, too bad, pardner! *Then* you would just have to spend your last days repenting of the wild ways which had brought you here; and hope that some celestial Wells Fargo would carry the news of this timely remorse to Headquarters, before you finally filed your claim for admittance to that Great Bar Room in the sky. Oh, ho! Those golden roulette-wheels and honky-tonk harps! Sure. A man wouldn't want to miss out on all that, would he? For without some such, Eternity would be as bleak as a Faro-dealer's eye; and nothing to get excited over at all.

But fortunately there was cash-in-poke a-plenty to support the middle-aged old-timer slogging out his last bare-knuckle bout with tuberculosis in the private room set aside for this purpose; gains ill-gotten and misspent for the most part, but that didn't trouble him so's you'd notice. No, his one problem was the probability that any moment now one of his old cronies would likely kick the door in, and try to beat the Grim Reaper to the draw – for he had many such over-ambitious friends.

So he awaited his well-earned end like the fine old Southern gentleman he used to be; a six-gun in one hand, in case of unwelcome health visitors, and a bottle of 'Rare Old Grandad' in the other, in case of sudden sobriety.

And meanwhile he was filling the flying time with a little target practice; to the discomfort of the hitherto flourishing population of resident cockroaches, who skipped and trembled accordingly. In fact, the terminal ward of Glenwood sounded like it had been hired for a reunion of the Wild Bunch; and I therefore paused somewhat diffidently before knocking on the door marked 'Quiet at all times'. After all, I had ridden several hundred miles to meet this particularly celebrated, inebriated invalid; and I didn't wish the journey to be wasted on account of my sudden decease. I mean, if you were a journalist in the last days of the Old West, you learned to be a little careful before insisting that the public has the right to know. There were a few characters still around who would give you an argument about a crack like that . . .

My name's Buntline, by the way – should have told you before; Ned Buntline – pleased to meet you. And, as you may have heard, I've made a certain amount of coin in my time biographising these same notorious characters for the edification of the reading fraternity. Fact is, I can honestly claim to have put Buffalo Bill Cody where he is today – but that's another story. Right now, I was on the track of one of the last colourful survivors of a vanishing era, as the saying is; and since truth must at all times be served, as another saying is, I eventually took advantage of a brief pause in all this justifiable pesticide, and rapped smartly on the splintered panels . . .

'Come in shootin', then; if you're comin',' coughed a raucous but well-modulated voice from within.

'I ain't armed,' I replied, 'so I fear I can't oblige.' And I stepped into the now tranquil room, to find myself looking down the open-for-business end of a large calibre Colt.

'Friend of Wyatt's' I announced hastily, 'called to pay my last respects.'

'Are you now? Well, in that case,' acknowledged Doc Holliday gracefully, sliding the shooter politely into a bunch of funereal lillies Bat Masterson had sent him, 'you'll have a drink with me . . .'

In view of my recent association with Wyatt Earp, you may think it strange that Doc and I had not previously locked horns? But you maybe know how it used to be on the old gamblers' circuit? Folks tended to leave cow-towns by night, and in opposing directions; and at this time – which, to be precise, was November 10, 1887 – Earp and Holliday had not met for several years. Busy in their very different ways, of course; and neither being much of a hand at the epistolary, as opposed to the pistolry, art, Doc had never even heard of me; so he was at a loss to account for my well-meant visitation; and, after a glass or two said so.

'Well,' I told him, notebook at the ready, 'it's about the O.K. Corral . . .'

'What about it?' asked Doc, reaching for his six-gun once more. 'You ain't also a friend of the Clantons, by any chance?'

I quickly denied any such ill-advised relationship.

'No,' I said, 'it's just that there's one or two things about that little fracas of yours and Wyatt's has always puzzled me some. I mean, why, for instance, does everyone say you used a shotgun? You never had before . . .'

'And I didn't then,' said Holliday, grinning like a friendly hyena into the neck of his bottle. 'Never utilised that class of instrument no how! No, sir. Why use a bone-saw when you can use a chisel, as I used to say when I was a dentist? No, that particular rumour is a dad-blasted lie!'

'Then *why* does everyone say . . . I mean, a twelve-bore ain't quite according to the code of combat, is it?'

'Calling me a liar?' he enquired pleasantly; preparing, it seemed, to fan a last hammer in a good cause.

'No, not for a moment!' I assured him. 'But, in that case, how'd the story get about?'

'It's a way stories have,' mused Holliday. 'Ain't it always the same? Do a friend a favour; and in no time you're known as a hooch-crazed killer with no kind of a social conscience. Why, I could happily massacre a man who said a thing like that! I could cut out his yellow liver with a Bowie knife!' he added, thinking about it. 'And then toss it to a hungry coyote; so's it'd pizen the crittur...' he concluded, with an air of having done justice all round.

Even so, a story is a story, so I was fool enough to pursue the matter. 'It's one of the things Wyatt wouldn't talk about,' I told him. 'Odd, that! You'd think he'd have been glad to put the record straight – seeing he was such a friend of yours.'

'Well, there's some things you *can't* really talk about – not if you don't truly understand them. Never talked about it myself, come to that... But now... Well, I guess it makes no never mind, this late in the game. You see,' he said, 'like I've been civil enough to tell you, though I never carried such a weapon myself, there was *another* Doctor at the O.K. Corral... and he *did*! Oh, by God, didn't he just!' chuckled Holliday. 'And that without any particular conception of accuracy, as I recall! Blasted the thing off every which way, like it was a Gatling gun mounted on a roulette wheel! And I tell you, Mr Buntline, that I, the great Doc Holliday, have never been so scared gutless in all my born days!

'Now, in case you're tempted to think,' he continued, 'that I am about to jeopardise my highly regarded immortal soul by some kind of falsehood, it seems to me I'd best explain about this other Doctor; before you give voice to the kind of disbelievin' sentiment as I'd have to kill you for! Seems I've enough blood on my boots without notching up another plea of self-defence on the very frontier of the Promised Land; where I hear they judge you a mite more vengeful than even Judge Bean used to, in the great days, West of the Pecos! So, if you'll jest sit there peaceable, and drink as much of the juice as you can accommodate like a gentleman, I'll do my damnedest to tell you how it all came about: and then, if you will, we can depart on our separate paths to Perdition, with everything fair and square between us ...

'So I take it, Mr Buntline, that at your tender age you may not have heard of time travel ... or even, so help me, of the TARDIS? Well, like I say, it ain't that easy to understand: but the TARDIS, if you'll kindly believe me, was – and is, for all I know – a kind of four-wheel buggy designed for ridin' every sort of direction through eternity, without much decent respect for the laws of physics. And this other Doctor feller I was tellin' you about, he drives it back an' forth through the star-spangled centuries, like it was a rodeo-bull got loose in Jackson's Hardware Store! It's a fact! Never seems to know quite where he'll land up next! And back in 1881, by golly, it was Tombstone, Arizona – where the poor old buzzard got hisself taken for me!'

At this point Doc Holliday broke off to remark that it was an unprintable pity if a dying man couldn't get a drink around here; so it would pleasure him some if I'd kindly oblige with the bottle ...

I passed him his cure-all; and was, in fact, happy to do so – because, from where I'd been swallowing, the brew tasted like a blend of panther-fat and snake-oil. And while he was occupied with it, I risked raising a doubtful eye-brow. I mean, time travel? And what was it – the TARDIS? *Another* Doctor? Oh, come *on*!

But still and all, this wasn't the sort of craven attempt to shuffle sideways out of responsibility that I could easily associate with John H. Holliday – or, leastways, with what I'd always heard about him. The coldest killer the West had ever seen – well, maybe. But always a gentleman with it, so Wyatt had told me. A man with a healthy dislike for facing the music; but never one to

12

deny that he'd written the tune; or called it, either, come to that! So why would he start trying to fool me at this time of his life? Or of his death, rather – because you could tell he wasn't long with us by the way his drink kept glazing over.

So I went on listening to his crazy-sounding story for the rest of that afternoon; while the whisky sank lower in the bottle – *and* in another he drew from a shoulder-holster, round about tea-time – until, you know, I finally believed him! Yes, sir, I did; and I make so bold as to hope that you will, too. Because it explains a deal of stuff that had just never seemed to add up in the other accounts I'd heard from so-called eye-witnesses – who'd probably never been nearer to the O.K. Corral than the railhead at Abilene!

And so, friends, here follows:

'A True and Full Account
of
The Gunfight at The O.K. Corral,
And of Events leading Thereto;
As told to me, Ned Buntline,
In the Terminal Ward of Glenwood Springs, Colorado,
by
Doctor John H. Holliday,
Dental Surgeon, Gambler, and Gun-Man,
Knife-Fighter, Con-Artist and Southern Gentleman.'

And Liar? Oh, surely not . . . !

1

Landfall in Tombstone

To hear Holliday tell it, life on board the TARDIS can't have been all candied yams and sassafras at the best of times; what with one thing and another, such as alien life forms cluttering up the cuspidors, and so forth. But when the Doctor had toothache, it became downright intolerable...

'It's no use,' he groaned, 'I simply have to find a dentist before we move another millenium!'

Steven and Dodo looked at each other in alarm. Difficult to find a decent one anywhere in an emergency – never mind a millenium... and *then* there'd probably be a waiting list.

'Haven't you got any pain-killers in the lab?' asked Steven. 'Something to tide you over till we get... wherever we're going?'

'My dear boy, amongst my supplies I have everything we could possibly need to counteract the effects of all death-rays from alpha to omega; devices for the instantaneous resetting of broken bones; and specifics to counteract cellular mutation... but for some reason I neglected to pack any aspirin! No, the tooth will just have to be extracted...'

'Shall I have a go?' said Dodo, helpfully. 'I once did a first-aid course at school... not very well, though...' she admitted.

'Certainly not!' snapped the Doctor. 'In any case, I'm sure the curriculum did not include the more sophisticated techniques of dental surgery. I fear there is nothing for it but to land at once.'

'Yes – but where?' said Steven.

'It doesn't matter!' the Doctor agonised. 'Wherever there is some form of vertebrate life, there will be teeth – and where there are teeth, there will be... oh... ouch!' And he reeled over to the control panel.

The dials wavered uncertainly. They'd been through all this before.

'But look here,' objected Steven, 'supposing there's only *in*-vertebrate life when we get there? It would be just like you to land us on Jupiter or somewhere, where everything's gaseous or liquid – you know, like those great, nebulous jelly-fish things we met on... where was it?... with poisonous what-nots...'

'*Don't!*' shuddered Dodo.

'Quite right, Dodo. Don't you presume to lecture me on intergalactic biology, my boy! I know perfectly well what I'm doing...!'

'Makes a pleasant change...!' muttered Steven, fortunately inaudibly.

In any case, the Doctor was already clutching at an apparently haphazard selection of levers with the air of a demented xylophonist, who finds he's brought along the wine list instead of the score.

'Don't you think,' said Dodo, without much hope, 'it would be better to wait until...?'

But whatever eventuality she anticipated, it was already too late. For the TARDIS had materialised.

* * *

They looked out upon an unprepossessing landscape. To start with, it was raining heavily. And even had it not been, the outskirts of Tombstone, Arizona in 1881, were not such as to qualify for an architect's award. Too little thought, the adjudicators would probably have felt, had been given to environmental considerations. Mind you, the town *did* blend in with its surroundings – but since these were of mud, that hardly constituted an advantage.

However, the Doctor was as jubilant as if he'd just discovered El Dorado, the shining city of legend; and furthermore, caught it living up to expectations in a big way.

'There you are!' he crowed. 'What did I tell you? Civilisation at last!'

'Civilisation?' Steven and Dodo sought unhopefully for some small evidence of Humanity's widely advertised rise from barbarism, and found it wanting.

With typical unerring accuracy, the TARDIS appeared to have homed in somewhere to the unsavoury rear of a disused livery stable – and one which had not been left entirely as a horse would wish to find it.

The place had atmosphere, all right; but they rather wished it hadn't. They could have breathed better in ... well, in the ammonia swamps of Alpha Centauri, for instance – and that was saying something!

Through the leaning door of the premises could be seen a distant, straggling vista of sagging shacks and sloping adobes, which even the shrewdest property speculator could only have described as offering ample scope for instant demolition. But if he ever had, then unfortunately he had found no takers. Because there it still stood, idling into corruption, like, as Steven put it, a souvenir copy of the Slough of Despond.

'Oh, come on, Steven,' said Dodo, 'at least we're back home . . .'

He looked at her in astonishment.

'So this is where you come from, is it? Explains a lot!'

'Oh, really!' she expostulated. 'Just for once, can't you try to look on the bright side?'

'Very well, you point to it – then I'll look at it. It'll be a pleasure!'

'At all events,' interrupted the Doctor, hastily, 'the inhabitants are obviously at an advanced stage of development . . .'

'I beg your pardon?'

'Look,' he said triumphantly, 'there's a wheel! At least they've discovered that!'

It would have been difficult for them not to. Quite a number of these triumphs of ingenuity lay about the place – most of them with spokes missing, but nonetheless indubitably wheels! *And* broken-down buggies, there were; *and* discarded horseshoes, wrapped in their own rust. The fact is, as you will have gathered by now, they had landed slap-bang in the middle of the O.K. Corral – and there was even a signboard, hanging sideways from one bent rail, to prove it.

'Whoopee!' said Dodo. 'We're in a Western!'

United for once, her two friends glared at her . . .

2

The Last Chance

And while all this was going on, life – or what passed for it – was moving on its sinister way through the thriving hell-hole about them.

For the three surviving Clanton boys were riding into town. Reading from major to minor, their names were Ike, Phineas and Billy – and they didn't care a damn who knew it! They wanted people to know, you hear? And to emphasise this point, Billy even went so far as to rear his horse in a way he'd seen it done somewhere, and fire his initials into the 'Gone to Lynching' sign on the sheriff's office. *Not* having seen it done anywhere, the horse sank to its haunches in a puddle, which rather spoiled the effect; but still, he'd made his point – and Ike clicked his tongue reprovingly.

'Now, why for d'you want to do a fool thing like that?' he enquired, tonelessly. 'Save your slugs for Doc Holliday, boy!'

'I ain't scared of Holliday,' asserted this junior all-American gun-slinger. 'Reckon I can take him any time!'

Impressed, Phineas parted his beard, and spoke through it. 'You hear that, Ike? Brother Billy here ain't scared! Haw! Haw!' he added, unkindly.

'Nobody said you was scared, boy; not that I recall. Brother Reuben, now, he weren't scared any. But that didn't stop Holliday fillin' him full of holes as a ...' He sought for a picturesque simile. He failed. 'As a lawyer's argument,' he ended, lamely.

Hopefully, Phineas changed the subject. 'So where do we meet up with Seth?' he enquired, wanting to know.

'Last Chance Saloon,' answered Ike, thereby bringing a lick to all lips, except those of Billy – always a sullen boy.

'What for we need the likes of Seth Harper?' he grumbled, 'I say we do the job ourselves.'

'Pa's payin' him, that's why. Pa says we work along with him. And what Pa says goes, rather than ...' he was still having trouble with his dénouements ... 'rather than what you say!' he finished, after some thought.

Dismounting, they entered the bar of the Last Chance Saloon – leaving their horses outside, as previously instructed on several occasions.

Perhaps a word here about this hostelry, famed though it may be in the lower class of obituary.

Well, it weren't no plush-lined sleep-easy, with a cactus-court cat-gut ensemble, that's for sure! And there weren't no picture of your genial host and his lady on the occasion of their silver wedding behind the bar, neither. On account, your host – by name of Charlie – weren't a mite genial; and his ladies came and went with monotonous irregularity.

No, what there was behind the bar, was a shot-up oil-painting of a fat blonde in her birthday rig. Sitting on a cloud, she was, being molested by a bunch of tear-away cherubs, who looked as if they'd been up several nights round a stud-game, and passing the nectar pretty free, at that.

It was that kind of place. Why, I declare, there used to be a song about it. Now, how did it go?

> With rings on their fingers
> And bells on their toes,
> The gals come to Tombstone
> In their high silk hose.
> They'll dance on the tables
> Or sing you a tune,
> For whatever's in your pocket
> At the Last Chance Saloon.

(And that's putting it a mite delicate, I'd say...)

> There's gamblers from Denver
> And guns from the South,
> And many a cow-poke
> With a bone dry mouth.
> So from midnight to morning
> The bar's going boom,
> Till there's blood upon the sawdust
> In the Last Chance Saloon!

Got the picture, have you? Right. So let's get back to the Clantons; who have just about disentangled themselves from the busted swing-doors by now, and spat out the fresh air they'd unavoidably inhaled on the way over...

Time they sashayed in, the place was a little on the empty side – and you couldn't blame it! Firstly, Charlie was still sweeping up the teeth left over from last night's hurrah; and, secondly, leaning on the bar as though it had given him some kind of argument, was a character of so villainous an appearance that you might have taken him for a film extra, waiting for an audition.

You'd have been wrong. This was the afore-mentioned Seth Harper; known to the sheriffs of five counties as portrait of the year. Not a top-class shootist, by no means; but say you wanted a friend shot in the back, and no questions asked, then he was your boy.

With some difficulty, he spoke. 'You took your sweet time gettin' here, Clanton. Holliday's rig pulled into town afore noon.'

Ike hated criticism. 'Rode out as soon as I got your wire figured,' he said. 'For Pete's sake – "Holiday in Tombstone"! There's two l's in our kind of Holliday. Thought at first it was from a tourist tout, or some such! Anyways, the Doc'll keep whiles a drink or three, I'd say . . .'

Billy swaggered forward, spoiling his effect once more – this time by some temporary problem with his spurs. 'Sure 'nough will. Charlie – four bottles, fast!'

Seeing how the party was likely to develop, Ike felt he'd best get on with the introductions. 'You boys know Snake-eyes Harper?' he enquired.

They nodded, and said 'Yup'. Seth didn't. 'Don't you ever call me Snake-eyes, you hear? Last man called me that lost one of his own!' And he blinked his scaly lids resentfully.

'What's he mean by that?' asked Phineas, slowly. 'I mean, when a man's got eyes like . . . I mean, seems only natural you'd call him . . . Well, wouldn't you?'

Ike intervened rapidly. 'Sure, Seth, sure . . . Phineas here is only funnin'. Now, come on, Seth – we're all friends here, ain't we? Now, ain't we all in this together?'

'You mean, *I'm* in it. Seems like you three's gonna be *together* – jest settin' at the ringside – an watchin'.'

'Now that ain't so, Seth,' said Phineas. 'We're backin' you – you know we are. *You* make your play, and then *we* gun him down. That's the way we planned it. Easy as skinnin' summer frogs!'

This went down very well. 'Summer frogs,' agreed Ike.

'Frogs, sure,' said Billy.

'Don't know about frogs,' said Seth, 'but you surely have got a way with words there. Okay then – frogs!' and he smiled for the first time. They hoped it would be the last. It showed his teeth.

So, a consensus having been reached, they slapped each other around a while; and then, still chuckling at Phineas the phrase-maker, they settled down to pass the time with a little light drinking.

And there, for the moment, it will be more pleasant to leave them . . .

3

The Brief Career of Dead-shot Steve

There ain't nothing like dressing the part, is there? And so our three time travellers eventually emerged into the quagmire of the Corral, as if for a provincial production of old Bill Cody's Road Show! Well, of course, you get conditioned by the cheaper sort of Western fiction, such as I have been known to write myself, on occasion; but still and all, you might have thought the foul reality of Tombstone would have modified their choice of costume somewhat... Never mind; when it comes to the Wild West, everyone is a boy at heart – except the girls, of course; and I expect they've got their own problems. Dodo was certainly in the way of acquiring a few, I'd say; wearing, as she had chosen to do, a little number made up of scarlet furbelows and flounces trimmed with black lace – the whole set off with a picture-hat of such dimensions that an enterprising florist could well have opened a branch department on a corner of its brim. Not to put too fine a point on it, she looked like the proprietress of a broken-down cat-house in one of the less select quarters of New Orleans; but when she prinked and preened in front of the Doctor, and asked his opinion, he contented himself with saying

'Absurd!' and left it at that. After all, you don't want to give needless offence; and, in any case, his tooth was still savaging him more than slightly.

So, with the merest, scarcely perceptible shudder, he turned to Steven, and asked why he had deemed it essential to disguise himself as Billy the Kid. 'Asking for trouble, I'd have thought,' he groaned. 'Why couldn't you have worn something inconspicuous, like I have done?'

Since the garments in question were, from North to South, a Mexican sombrero, an eye-shattering fancy gambler's weskit, inadequately concealed by a velvet box-back coat, and yellow whip-cord breeches, tucked into silver-ornamented riding boots, Steven forbore to answer the question; but assured the Doctor that he was quite well able to look after himself, thank you, when it came to a show-down.

'Stranger,' he snarled, in an accent which seemed to have originated in the region of the Okefenokee Swamp, 'I guess you don't know who I is? Folks call me Dead-shot Steve. Moreover, my daddy was a bull-alligator, an' I can wrastle my own weight in cougars!'

To prove this contention, he drew two pearl-handled revolvers, and twirled the surprised weapons by their trigger guards. Very impressive! Or would have been, if they hadn't immediately been shot from his hands by a party who had approached unnoticed, and been an interested audience to the foregoing.

A tall man, he was; lean, and with the flickering hell-fire eye of a misogynistic Methodist preacher. He leant over the sway-back of a skeletal horse, as though it was the pulpit rail of the last tin chapel left standing in Gomorrah; and in his black-gloved hand was a smoking pistol with a twelve-inch barrel – as I know, because I designed and gave it to him long ago in Dodge City. He was, they were glad to see, smiling – but only as if the joke was something private between him and Jehovah.

Nevertheless – 'Hey!' quavered Steve, in a reproachful manner; 'That hurt!'

'What is the meaning of this?' demanded the Doctor.

'You want to find out,' drawled the newcomer, 'then try movin' sudden... Now, git over there agin' the wall... real slow, mind...'

Well, you do, don't you, in a situation like that? But the Doctor resented his attitude, all the same.

'I don't know who you are, sir; or by what right...'

'State Marshal's my right, and Wyatt Earp's my name.'

'Wyatt Earp?' choked Dodo.

'Something wrong, ma'am?' queried Wyatt, tipping his hat.

'No – it's just that... well, I've always wanted to meet you... and now, here we are – face to face!'

'The Lord surely do work in mysterious ways, don't He? And now He's seen fit to make us acquainted, perhaps you an' your friends'll oblige both Him and me by steppin' along to the sheriff's office, down along the street a-piece? So's you can identify yourselves to Bat Masterson in a decent, law-abidin' manner?'

'Now wait a minute,' said Steven; 'perhaps I'd better explain. Actually, you see, I'm not really a gunfighter at all...'

'That's kind of obvious, boy. That's why I'm doin' you a real courtesy by takin' you in...'

'But why?' asked Steven, thinking he'd cleared the matter up rather well. 'I can see no reason...'

'On account, boy, as I jest heard the Clanton boys are in town; an' that makes it kind of unhealthy for a stranger who claims he's the fastest man in the territory. So you can jest pick up them shiny new toys of yours, there, an' get movin'...'

And so, of course, they moved...

4

A Funeral is Arranged

During our absence, the decor of the Last Chance has been improved considerably by the addition of the resident chanteuse – a lady with the unfortunate name of Big-nose Kate Elder. But what's in a name, as someone says, somewhere? Just be grateful that a young woman with enough bounce, personality, and zip to hold down a job in such a cess-pit, is prepared to pound the ivories for our entertainment while the following conversation ensues. To which, I may say, she also listens.

Ike was holding the floor; as though he thought he'd caught it moving. 'Holliday cain't be *that* good,' he opined, 'it jest ain't possible! Against the four of us? He won't know what hit him!'

'Now that'd be a real shame,' said hot-shot Billy. 'I'd like for him to know. I'd like him to know us for Reuben's brothers. That way,' he explained, 'he'll realise he's been overtaken by... what's that Greek guy's name? Used to overtake people... Nemmy someone... Yeah, Nemmy – I got it – Sis!'

'You addressin' me?' snarled Seth, always quick to resent an implication.

'No – it was some Greek, I tell you!'

'*Some* Greek, *I'll* say!' chorused his loyal brothers, not quite sure which away the talk was drifting.

Seth wasn't either. He wiped his hand with the back of his mouth.

'Now see here,' he said, 'can we get back to the subject? Now listen,' he added, changing his instructions at the last moment, 'you boys don't *know* Holliday! You mean, you want *him* to come lookin' for *us*? When you ain't never even *seen* him? If so, you're crazy as a . . . as a . . .'

'Jay-bird?' suggested Phineas. 'Or maybe, a frog?' he added, anxious to repeat his former triumph.

'Well, one of the two, anyway,' agreed Seth. 'Hey, what is it with you an' frogs? You some kind of pervert?'

As always, Ike got him out of it. 'Well, not *that* kind,' he said. 'You and your fantasies stay out of this, can't you, Phin? So where *is* Holliday now?'

'How in hell should *I* know?' grumbled Seth; 'I ain't runnin' no general information service, am I? All I *do* know is what I heard – that he rode in this morning.'

'Now just let me get this straight,' said Phineas, unabashed. 'You mean, *you* never seen him neither? Land sakes, I thought that was why you came along . . . so's you could . . .'

'I don't *need* to see him,' interrupted Seth. 'I heard him described – and I seen pictures. Dapper little feller, in a black velvet, box-back coat, an' a fancy gambler's vest.'

You see? Plenty of scope for future misunderstandings.

'So fine!' said Billy. 'So we know him when we find him. So *how* do we find him?'

'We don't *have* to find him. You boys never heard of

Holliday's drinkin' an' gamblin'? So where's the only place in town he can do both?'

The boys nodded, sagely. 'Right here,' they concluded.

'So then, we jest sit here – maybe havin' us another little drink – an' we wait for him . . . an' then we blast him! That's all we gotta do . . . Easy as . . . as . . .'

'Bakin' a possum in a pie?' enquired Phineas, tentatively.

This was a new one, at any rate – and they thumped each other some more.

While Kate, who could do more than play a mean piano, let me tell you, spoke to Charlie. 'I'll be right back, Charlie' was what she said.

'Why, where you fixin' to go?' enquired her employer, likewise speaking for the first time.

'Jest thought me of an errand I forgot,' she explained, plausibly.

'Well, you better be back right smart – if you aim to keep on workin' here!'

'Why, of course I will, Charlie . . .' And she made a splendid exit.

A simple conversation, you may think? But significant, as events will prove.

5

Notice to Quit

You see, it was precisely at this time in his life, so Doc Holliday told me, that he had decided to get married for once; and likewise settle down – if, that is, the lady was going to insist on it. And to this end, he was even now installing a handsome dentist's chair, complete with all the trimmings a lady loves, in his new premises on Main Street, Tombstone.

'Easy there!' he said to the Wells Fargo delivery boys, 'You hear me? You carry that there piece of merchandise real gentle – like she was a one-day bride!'

His mind right set on domesticity, you will note? And I'll tell you for why. In some fly-bitten cow-town down the circuit a-piece, he had recently had occasion to shoot the bejesus out of one Reuben Clanton – of whom we have already heard so much.

Some trifling altercation of an academic nature – in fact, as to just how many aces a man can reasonably be expected to have up his sleeve at the one time; *that* was the point at issue between them which had caused the argument. And, as usual, Doc had won it. Fair enough, you will likely say; and, on account of the sporting ethic prevailing at the time, I agree.

But the said Reuben Clanton had friends in town, and they didn't see it our way. They objected to the luck of the quick draw, and demanded a ballot. The outcome of which was that Doc should be strung as high as convenient forthwith, if not sooner.

It was about then that Big-nose Kate had the delicate female initiative to set fire to the saloon; thereby distracting the interested parties for long enough so she and Doc whom she admired, could depart for points West.

Well, after all, that's the sort of thing a lady will do – especially if the feller in question hasn't yet paid her for his previous night's entertainment and lodging; and Doc was as grateful as a man should rightly be under the circumstances.

Moreover, seeing as he had carelessly left his money-belt back in the conflagration, he considered the only honourable course open to a Southern gentleman was to propose marriage to his fair rescuer, in lieu of lucre.

It was a proposition she duly accepted with some gratitude – and a lot of surprise; because such a slap-me-down suggestion had never come her way before. Johnny Ringo had never made it, for one; nor Jesse James for another. Oh, and several more prominent citizens – none of them had.

But Holliday was different; and he figured a gentleman gotta do what another sort of man would run a mile from – that's all.

So there he was, this wild, free spirit, feathering the love-nest with gew-gaws, fal-lals, and a certain amount of hooch, when the sound of size nine high-button boots in a tearing hurry indicated the approach of his intended...

'Doc, I gotta talk to you!' she panted.

He rubbed his chin, thoughtfully. 'Well, now, yes, of course I'd taken that into consideration, Kate – and decided as I'm prepared to go along with it. Sure, I know matrimony ain't all kisses an' such. There'll be those long evenings, with you yapping an' me jest settin' there. You have to take the rough with the smooth, from what I'm told . . .'

'Doc, will you listen?'

'Why, I jest finished tellin' you, Kate – I don't rightly see no alternative.'

'Damn your hide, I mean *now*! Doc, I thought you promised me as you was goin' to give up gun-play? You said you was goin' to hang up your two Colt specials, your Derringer, your knife, and your Sharpe's Buffalo rifle over the whisky-still, right next to Ma's likeness!'

'Now that there truly is an offensive weapon, sure 'nough! But I aim to keep my word, Kate. Hereon in, my lightnin' fingers are gonna be applied to molars, canines, and the like. I'm all through with blood and pain.'

'Is that so? In that case, Doc, you'd better clear out of Tombstone right now!'

Understandably, he evidenced surprise, not unmixed with irritation.

'But, tarnation blazes, I only just got here! What ails you, Kate? You fixin' to renage on our lovin' agreement? You been rollin' them oglin' eyes at some other man? You met someone else already?'

'I met four of 'em, if you want to know. An' they're a-layin' for you right now back in the bar!'

'The hell you say! Who are these gentlemen? Anyone of my acquaintance?'

'Three of 'em's the Clanton brothers.'

He sighed deeply. 'Now ain't it always the same?

Won't that family never learn? Seems like every varmint I kill's got a passel of brothers waiting to join him! So who's the fourth, may I ask?'

'Gun-slinger name of Seth Harper. He's ugly, Doc – he's real ugly.' She considered this statement a while, then amended it as follows: 'Doc, he's *awful* ugly!'

'Well, I ain't plannin' to shack up with him, Kate. Snake-eyes Harper? Why, from what I hear, he's nothin' but a side-winding, back-shooting, natural son of a three-toed tree-toad! Guess that about covers it. Now, if there's one thing makes me real angry, it's that class of animal steppin' out of its league! Reckon I'll have me a little talk with him to that effect.'

'You're all through bein' angry, Doc. An' if you won't leave town, you gotta promise me you'll stay out of the Last Chance till they blow over. Won't take long at that, the way they're drinkin' . . .'

'Now, that don't appeal, Kate, that don't come at all natural. Comes the day I can't step into a saloon for a thimble of dry sherry, it'll be my liver stops me – not a bunch of boozed-up hoodlums!'

'I'll stop you, Holliday, if I have to,' said a third, gravel-filtered voice, joining the discussion uninvited. Fortunately, Doc recognised it, and put his Derringer back where it belonged. 'Well, well,' he said, 'the *big* man! I was wondering when you'd show up, Masterson.'

'Soon as I heard you was in town,' croaked Bat, 'I figured it was time to tell you to get the hell out of it.'

'Now, why is everyone so goddam friendly so sudden? I tell you Sheriff, I'm a respectable tradesman now – a professional practitioner of the orthodontic art. I got no quarrel with anybody, have I, Kate?'

'Not that I've heard,' simpered Goody-Two-Boots, primly.

34

'Well then, keep out of trouble for one; jest stay in your hygienic, sweat-shop surgery, an' we'll get along fine.'

'Why, Bat, I was just about to enter same. And I surely do look forward to the pleasure of entertainin' you in my sparklin' new chair real soon. Don't leave it too long, you hear? There's a couple of things about your mouth I don't like the look of; never have done, come to that. Will you take my arm, Miss Catherine, or shall I have someone carry you over the threshold?'

And the engaged couple entered the marital waiting-room; leaving Bat Masterson to wonder what Holliday had meant about his mouth. What didn't he like about it? Surely not his moustache, of which he was proud. As would have been a walrus.

He resolved to take the matter up with the dentist at their next meeting; and fingering the treasured growth protectively, he squelched back to his office.

Where he found company.

6

Identity Parade

The gaunt Earp had finally established our three
jazzily bedizined time travellers in adjacent cells; where
they were examining the facilities with ill-concealed
distaste.

'If you don't let us out of here at once,' the Doctor had
warned him, 'I shall have no alternative but to apply for
writs of habeas corpus – and see how you like that!'

'Well, this here's the Ritz of many a happy corpse,
right enough,' replied their captor, making a rare
attempt at humour; 'but you ain't leavin' it till you see fit
to tell me who you are an' where you come from.'

And since this, of course, was a thing almost
impossible to explain to the uninitiated, the conversation had then reached its long-awaited impasse; and the
monolithic Marshal had returned to his gloomy perusal
of some of the snappier items contained in the Book of
Revelations. The bit about the Great Beast, he'd always
rather liked. Put him in mind of his horse, Apocalypse..

Bat was pleased to see him; but didn't at once say so.
Not out of any churlishness – even though Wyatt *was* in
his chair – but because when strong men meet, words
are sometimes unnecessary between them. And then

there's the matter of vocabulary, too. I mean, 'Hallo,' is somehow inadequate; and 'Gee, fella, am *I* glad to see *you*?' seems to be overdoing things rather. No, difficult. Very.

So for a while there was silence between them, while Bat accidentally rolled his moustache into a cigarette, and Wyatt merely murmured the occasional 'Hallelujah!' in his purring, harmonium-like voice.

At length – 'I thought you was out lookin' for the Rudabaugh Bunch?' said Bat.

'I found 'em,' said Wyatt. 'There will be wild rejoicin' in Hell this very day; and for a twelve-month after, I shouldn't wonder. Glory be to the power of the Lord!' he added.

'What?' said Bat.

'Amen!' said Wyatt.

'Oh,' said Bat. He cleared his throat, and fiddled with his badge.

'Don't do that,' said Wyatt; 'makes me nervous...'

He didn't *look* nervous; but there you are – you never can tell...

'And is that some of 'em you got in the cage there?' asked the Sheriff.

After all, it was *his* gaol, and someone had to do the paper work...

'No,' said Wyatt. 'Them's just an uppity parcel of vagrants, as I took into protective custody till such time as they see fit to give a proper account of theirselves. Question 'em careful, Bat – question 'em real shrewd! Could be trouble. The hosts of Midian sure is out a-prowlin', this blessed day.'

'Blessed, you call it?' said Bat, glancing out of the window; 'I've seen better days, I must say.'

'No-one lasts forever,' agreed Wyatt.

Bat ignored the remark.

'And that bunch don't look particular dangerous, do they now?' he continued. 'I mean, they ain't by no means the Daltons. More like as if they was actors from the Bird Cage Theatre, I'd say. Eddie Foy's playin' there at the moment,' he remembered. 'Get you a ticket?'

'Theatres,' reproved Wyatt, 'is a haunt of vice an' corruption. Lewdness an' filth.'

'Well, the notices *were* good,' said Bat.

And the Doctor, who had been listening with interest, at once adopted the cover so conveniently offered.

'Quite so,' he interjected. 'That, indeed, is who we are – a humble troupe of travelling players...'

'Then why didn't you say so before?' demanded Wyatt.

'You yourself have just explained why. We are commonly regarded as rogues and vagabonds. Incorrectly, of course, but experience has taught us to be wary of revealing our true profession, before we are certain of our reception. Moreover, we are at the moment between engagements; and as always, rather loth to admit it. But now that your colleague had seen through our modest deception, allow me to perform the introductions: Miss Dodo Dupont – Queen of the Ivory Keys; Mr Steven Regret – Songs for All Occasions; and lastly, your humble servant, Doctor... Doctor Caligari – Master of Magic and Legerdemain!'

'Doctor who?' enquired Bat.

'Precisely!' said the Doctor; and he looked at the others for approval. He was disappointed, of course – but he was used to that by now.

'And if there *are* any tickets going,' said Dodo, 'we'd love to see Eddie Foy!'

'No, we wouldn't,' contradicted the Doctor. 'In fact, our sole purpose in visiting your fair city is so that I can avail myself of the services of a dentist. Perhaps one of you gentlemen would be so kind as to recommend one?'

'Well, now – ain't that something?' said Bat. 'Ain't that jest the daddy of all coincidences? Ain't that the livin', breathin' cock-a-mamie circumstance to beat all? Why, I'll be swiped sideways for an egg-stealin' polecat, if . . .'

'Keep it short, Bat,' warned Wyatt.

'. . . if it ain't!' his friend concluded.

'You all through now?'

'Jest about. But Wyatt, seems like an Act of Providence . . .'

'Reckon I'd know best about a thing like that. What are you trying to say?'

'Why, Wyatt . . .'

'An' don't say "Why, Wyatt!" Told you before – sounds like you're stammerin'. Man stammers, he's scared. An' a scared sheriff's a dead one. Go on!'

'Give me a moment . . . O.K. then, *listen* Wyatt – how about that? Guess who blew into town this morning!'

'Can't rightly say . . .'

'Why –'

'Careful!'

Bat took a deep breath. 'Holliday blew, that's who! That no-account, four-flushing, treacherous rattlesnake of a . . .'

'You're speakin' of a friend of mine?'

'That's right. Well he's opened himself a dental extractory, right here on Main Street! How about that? An' I was just goin' to run him out of town on a rail!'

'Oh, don't do that!' begged the Doctor. 'Or not until I've seen him anyway!'

'Feller's right, Bat,' said Wyatt. 'Like it or not, you an' me'll likely be needin' Holliday's assistance right soon. The way things are, we gonna thank the Lord for all the guns we can get!'

'Guns?' enquired the Doctor. 'I thought you said he was a dentist?'

'Time to time he is. Othertimes, he's the deadliest, alcoholic killer as ever saved my life. Down in Tucson, that was ... O.K. then, stranger – if that's truly your business in town, I won't keep you from it. If he gets a customer straight off, maybe he'll stick around a while. Let 'em out, Bat.'

The Doctor was probing his mouth cautiously. 'Homicidal, you say? And dipsomania, too? In that case, I'm not entirely sure that I need ... ouch ... his services ...'

'Don't worry, old timer,' comforted Wyatt. 'Doctor John H. Holliday don't ever mix business with misery. He'll do you a right good job, if you tell him I sent you ... an' if he's sober, of course. Which this hour he'll likely still be ... Now, on your way!'

So, in as little time as it took Bat Masterson to find the right key, the three friends were released on probation; and stumbled out on to Main Street, to go and meet their customary come-uppance.

7

Open Mouth Surgery

Seems they found the dentefactor's premises without any trouble – and that was something they should have made the most of, while they had the chance; being as how we all need just such an occasional tranquil moment in our lives.

Doc Holliday had chosen to advertise his whereabouts with the simple but striking device of a king-size, hardwood, decayed tooth; suspended over the sidewalk from an ornamental iron bracket – painted bright red, to simulate the appearance of a bleeding gum. Not only effective, I'd say, but also positively therapeutic; because one glance persuaded the Doctor that his pain resulted from nothing but an inflamed imagination.

'It was only the merest twinge,' he said. 'Undoubtedly psychosomatic in origin. No, I really don't think I need trouble the man over such a paltry . . . *ouch*!'

'You get in there, Doctor!' said Steven, ruthlessly. 'Now you've dragged us all into this god-forsaken hole, you'll damn well have the thing out. Otherwise there'll be tears and tantrums all the way to the next time warp!'

'You wouldn't dare to speak to me like that, my boy, if I weren't . . .'

'Probably not. So just think how nice it'll be to get your own back, once it's all over. Then Dodo and I will be able to play and sing at your convalescence, won't we? Honestly – the Queen of the Ivory Keys! Songs for All Occasions! We're not going to forgive you for that in a hurry!'

'Well, I had to say something . . .'

'Yes, you always do, don't you? Well, I only hope someone asks you to wow the town with a few conjuring tricks, and perhaps that'll be a lesson to you!'

'You are entirely heartless!'

'Of course we're not,' put in Dodo. 'Don't worry – it'll soon be over. And to show you how much we really love you, Steven and I will go on to the nearest hotel, and book three rooms and an enormous meal.'

'Yes,' said Steven. 'So you can just think of that, while you're screaming with agony in there. It will take your mind off things . . .'

'Very well. I honestly think I'd rather face a murderous, drunken dentist, than listen to you two in this mood. If I am spared, I will join you later . . .'

And he lurched into the shop – a very gallant gentleman . . . Dodo giggled – and Steven looked at her with some concern.

'I can't see there's a great deal to laugh at,' he said.

'Well, I was just thinking,' spluttered the callous hoyden, 'I hope he isn't expecting an anaesthetic. They haven't been invented yet!'

And slapping each other merrily, like a touring version of 'The Clanton Boys at Home', they set off for the Last Chance Saloon.

The Doctor's first impression of the premises was better

than he had been led to tremble at, by Wyatt's laconic encomium. To begin with, the place was fairly clean, because, after all, it hadn't been used yet. On the table in the waiting-room was a fairly recent selection of 'Wanted' notices for him to browse through; and also a few back numbers of 'Headstone Highlights', Tombstone's crusading weekly news-sheet.

'Mad Dog Killer To Stand For Mayor' announced a surprisingly bold headline. Ah well, most mushroom towns have a little trouble getting off the ground – and apparently its previous mayor had experienced the same difficulty.

'Popular incumbent to be planted on Boot Hill', began the article; 'where he can be confidently expected,' it continued, 'to fertilise the cactus with as much dedication as he has previously shown in Ma Golightly's establishment of a Saturday night, where he was a valued client.

'He departed this life, mourned by some, in Crum's Alley on Thursday last, Pa Clanton officiating. Interviewed by our Social Correspondent, Pa later said that although he did not seek high office, he would be glad to accept it on the usual terms – thought to be drinks on the house in perpetuity at the Last Chance Saloon.'

The Doctor read this titillatory 'chat-piece' with some misgiving; and having skipped lightly through the kangaroo-court circular, and the annoucements of forthcoming shot-gun weddings, he flung the periodical aside with a muttered 'Tut!', and proceeded to explore further.

The surgery in which he presently found himself did little to calm his qualms; but he fancied it would serve, in his present predicament. After all, you don't expect to find a Temple of Hygiene in a cow-town; and you are right not to.

But there was at least a comfortable looking chair – which he was not to know had previously seen service in the Death House at San Quentin – and adjacent to it, on a splintered saw-bench, lay a selection of curious instruments, gleaming, it seemed to him, with anticipation. In fact, there was everything a festered tooth could wish for – except a dentist to manipulate these macabre devices, prominent amongst which, he now noticed, was a brace and bit.

Groaning, he crossed the room and opened yet another door, which he presumed led to the living-quarters. They proved, however, to be the sleeping-quarters – and they were currently being used as such by the surgeon; and a lady who could only be, or so the Doctor supposed, the receptionist; who resented his intrusion, and said so.

In fact, Doc Holliday went so far as to produce a six-gun from beneath the pillow, and ask if the Doctor thought he was some kind of dad-blasted purity enforcement officer from the Band of Hope – because, if so, they could settle the matter right now.

But the Doctor explained his business; and, in practically no time at all, the misunderstanding was resolved to general satisfaction. Because, as Kate pointed out, he was their very first customer – and she further urged both Doctors not to be in the least bit nervous on that account, because she would be watching the whole thing, ready to lend a hand if need be.

As one Doctor, they discouraged this idea.

'Now Kate,' said Holliday, 'you know you cain't stand violence an' such; as you never leave off telling me. So kindly get right back in bed where you belong, and don't emerge till the ruckus is over. Won't take no more than a moment, once I've put the gentleman at his ease.'

'And how do you propose to do that?' quavered the Doctor.

'Well now, I'll tell you; you can either have a slug of rot-gut...'

The patient proclaimed his temperance principles.

'Or I can give you a little tap on the parietal with my equaliser. The choice is entirely yours.'

Although reassured to some extent by the use of the word 'parietal', which argued at least the rudiments of a medical background, the Doctor nevertheless discarded for the nonce his afore-mentioned prohibitionist views, and opted for the former alternative. Emboldened by which, he then enquired if Holliday was entirely sure what he was about.

'Never tolerated a complaint in my whole life, sir,' the practitioner boasted. 'Now, if you'll kindly stop your distracting cacophany, and open your goddam mouth real wide, I'll proceed to go for your gums.'

And he reached a trembling hand for the surgical wrench.

8

An Offer Refused

The Last Chance Saloon was really jumping by now –
and with some justification. It was a nervous place at the
best of times, and this wasn't one of them. The boys had
at last run out of conversation; and since none of them
felt like going out to fetch some more, they were
presently engaged in shooting the neck off any bottle
which had offended them by being empty.

Charlie had, in fact, mentioned that he didn't want no
trouble; but they had assured him that it weren't no
trouble at all, and continued to prove it, punctuating
their explosive obbligato with those high-pitched
yipping cries, which were such an attractive feature of
the Old West. Rather like Professor Barnstorm's
Musical Dogs in rehearsal, it was.

Speaking of music, Charlie explained to them that, if
there was any kind of professional integrity round here,
Kate would shortly be returning to continue her
selections from the classics; and they agreed that they
would look forward to that, then. But meanwhile they
would continue to provide their own entertainment, if
that was all right by him?

After a quick calculation of the odds, Charlie

supposed it was; and retreated to his thankless sanctum, where there was a picture of Lily Langtry he was fond of. 'What a Jersey Lily!' it was his habit to say; after which he would laugh. But right now, he was unable to summon so much as a snigger to his blue and mirthless lips. He wondered whether to pass the time with a little shaving, since it was a Friday; but decided against it, on the grounds that the mortician would no doubt take care of all that, in due course.

But these valedictory musings were cut short by the unexpected tolling of the bar-bell; and he emerged once more, to find that two strangers had been fool enough to enter his premises.

These, of course, were Steven and Dodo, who, having scoured the town – which could use it – for a Waldorf Astoria, had now decided that this must be where the action was. And they were right. Their entrance had not gone unobserved.

'Why, look-ee here,' said Ike.

'Why, look-ee here,' followed Phineas, admiring the phrase, 'if it ain't Calamity Jane an' Sam Bass!'

'Haw! Haw!' said Billy, to show he could appreciate a joke, 'well, if it jest ain't!'

Seth said nothing, to imply he was a loner, who always made up his own mind, when he could find it. But somehow he didn't think they were right.

And Charlie, who had his custom to think of, said 'What'll it be, stranger?' – an opening gambit he had always found to be much appreciated by the casual caller. But not this time. It wasn't Charlie's day.

'Nothing to drink, thank you,' said Steven, primly, 'but I'd like to book three rooms for the night, please . . .'

Charlie counted the passing trade, cautiously. 'For the two of you?' he enquired.

'They need one for a rumpus room, maybe?' suggested Ike.

'That's right – for funnin' an' such,' explained Phineas.

'Some place they can meet real private,' said Billy, offensively.

'A friend will be joining us later,' said Steven, anxious to dispel any prurient speculations at the outset. 'He's been held up.'

'Who hasn't, these days?' asked Charlie, with a malevolent glance at his regulars. 'Sign of the rotten times! Well then, I guess I'll have to get you to affix your labels to the book here . . .' And he pushed the mildewed volume towards them. 'Jest so's I can get in touch with the next of kin,' he explained. 'If need be . . .'

He breathed heavily over Dodo's shoulder, wilting a flower or so, and regarded her particulars with interest – if you follow me.

'Say,' he said, impressed, 'you really a piano player, lady?'

'You're durn tootin', I am!' said the irrepressible Dodo. ' "Queen of the Ivory Keys" – that's me!'

Steven groaned, and completed his own formalities.

'An' you're a sure 'nough singer, friend?' continued Charlie. 'Well, I'll be hog-tied for a booze-breathin' son of a prairie-oyster! That's what I'll be!'

'Why?' asked Steven, concerned on his behalf.

'Because in that case, I might jest be able to offer the pair of you a job! You see,' he explained, 'I got no regular pianist on account of he played me sour a mite too often, an' . . . well, he's kinda restin' right now . . .'

'Real peaceful,' agreed Seth, who had assisted at the ceremony.

'An' the little lady who's been fillin' in for him is a

touch unreliable. Well, I don't want to be hard, but she's got her other interests, I reckon...'

'Surely has,' said Seth, remembering one star-spangled night in Ground Hog's Hollow. 'Oh, boy!' he added, reflectively.

'So you see how it is?' concluded Charlie. 'Right now, I'm stuck for music as a porcupine on a pianola!'

A confusing thing to envisage, perhaps; but they got his drift – and Steven checked it before it became irreversible...

'Well, that's really very kind of you,' he appreciated, 'but I'm afraid the fact is, we shall have to leave first thing in the morning...'

'At sun-up,' translated Phineas, helpfully.

Disappointed, Dodo kicked Steven's ankle. 'But surely one night wouldn't make... wouldn't make no never mind, would it?' she cajoled, dropping into the vernacular. 'I've always wanted to be a gin-palace tootsie!'

'Certainly not!' snapped Steven. 'You know perfectly well, the Doctor would never allow it!'

The boys slumped upright, and cocked their ears like so many slack-whiskered lynxes. And a strange effect it was, to be sure. But no matter...

'You hear what I heard?' rumbled Ike, *blotto voce*.

'We heard!' corroborated the rest.

'Well, let me know if'n you change your minds,' said the disappointed impresario. 'The coffin's always open, like they say...'

'Is it?' said Dodo. 'Well, in that case, if you'll just give this key to our friend, the Doctor, when he arrives, we will retire to our rooms...'

And thereby hammering the last nail into said coffin, they swept up the Grand Staircase – something which had not previously been done in a coon's age . . .

With their departure there was a necessary pause for thought.

'So the Doc ain't travellin' alone this time,' reasoned Ike finally.

'Let me see that register!' said Billy.

'Now, boy, you know you cain't read,' objected Phineas. 'Give it here!'

Since he laboured under a similar disability himself, he passed the book to Ike, who had been to reform school.

'Steven Regret,' the scholar laboriously enunciated. 'Now there's a thing! Any of you boys ever seen a singer totin' six-guns afore?'

'Heard some who should have,' contributed Seth.

'Well, well, well – so Holliday's got hisself a partner,' pursued Ike. 'What I mean is,' he continued, for the benefit of the slower witted, 'he's got company! Now I don't know about you boys, but I'm surely goin' to have a itchy feelin' in the back of my neck, if Regret's comin' downstairs behind us, when the Doc comes through them doors.'

'In front of us,' reasoned Phineas.

'You got it!' said Ike.

'So why don't one of you,' said Seth, the strategist, 'go an' bring Regret down here again? So's we can keep an eye on him,' he clarified.

'Good thinking,' said Billy. 'On your way, Phin.'

'What'll I tell him?' asked his brother. 'I mean, I don't hardly know him . . .'

'Tell him,' said Ike, 'we'd take it as a personal favour if he was to give us a song before chow time. On account of ... say this ... say that we have been riding the range, and far removed from cultural distractions, since we can't remember when. That'll fetch him.'

'Bound to,' agreed Seth. 'You know what these here artistes is like. Give 'em any excuse, an' they sets to warblin' like a ... like a ...'

'Summer frog?' returned Phineas. They ignored him. The time for that sort of thing was long gone. Hereon in, it was serious.

'An' while Phin's takin' care of that little matter,' pursued Ike, sternly, 'you take a mosey down Main Street, Seth, an' see if you cain't find Holliday. I'm gettin' a mite tired of jest settin' here, waitin' ... I've had enough!'

'You surely have,' agreed Seth; and he high-tailed it for the Great Outdoors, before Ike could work that one out.

9

A Pardonable Error

Gun-slingers who mosey down Main Streets, are –
thank God! – a breed apart; and it suits them. They do
not, that is to say, simply walk from point A to point B,
same like you or I would do, if there was anything in it
for us. No, they prefer to zig-zag about, like a graph of
the trade figures in a bad month; occasionally spinning
on their heels and snarling, before dropping on to their
stomachs and rolling over and over to the nearest horse-
trough – where they can lie, breathing deeply, until
ready to proceed.

It is a strange discipline they follow: and one which
would likely lead to their being hauled off to the nearest
laughing-academy – were it not, of course, for the fact
that they are armed to the teeth, and would resent any
such interference with their liberty.

Well, it's a free country, as you may have heard; and so
the citizens of Tombstone were generally prepared to
take the broad view, and let them get on with it. After
all, it's their own clothes they're ruining, ain't it? And if a
man can't roll in the horse-flop whenever he feels that
way, what is our fair land coming to?

And so Seth Harper attracted little but that modicum

of attention required to avoid stepping on him, as he ducked and weaved through the weekday shoppers, like a play-pool dinghy rounding Cape Horn in a cyclone. And pretty soon, in the course of this routing, he fetched up against Holliday's shop-front; where he stood for a moment, frozen, as they say, into immobility, before cautiously swivelling his unpleasant head on its point of attachment, and peeking narrowly through the window.

And what did he see? Why, a dapper little man in a velvet, box-back coat, and a fancy gambler's vest; whose face may have been partly obscured for the moment by a blood-stained bandana clapped to the jaw, but who otherwise fitted the description so lovingly itemised by the police artists of several South-Western states.

There could, so Seth reasoned, be no mistake: this was the notorious rattle-snake of the Wild Frontier, the living legend himself, Doc Holliday. Besides, the man's name was above the door, weren't it? And if that didn't clinch the matter beyond all reasonable doubt, what, he would like to know, could?

He was wrong, of course; but can perhaps be forgiven under the circumstances. And the stress of emotion too – don't forget that! Emotions were a thing he wasn't used to – and they had taken their toll. Because, having been so often told about them, he knew his limitations; and he wasn't by no means about to push things to a fatal conclusion with *that* one – not all on his own. No, sir! I mean, come *on*!

So, summoning what he supposed to be a friendly smile from somewhere, and with hands akimbo, well away from his gun-belt, he sauntered into the shop...

As you will have gathered, Doc Holliday himself had

retired from the scene briefly, shortly after completing his miracle of modern surgery; ostensibly to show the decayed ivory trophy to Kate; but in fact to avail himself of a bracing snort, for he had been much shaken by the encounter, and bitten painfully on the thumb to boot!

No hard feelings, of course – all in the line of professional duty, but still... a man needs a quiet moment to work out the bill after an experience like that. And he had decided that, in all fairness, it should be extortionate!

So the Doctor was alone when the Terror of the Plains made his entrance, and prepared to speak. This was the bit Seth always dreaded – words! God, how he hated them! Nevertheless, he tried one for size...

'Doc?' he enquired.

The Doctor leaped like a bee that has sat on its sting. He knew few people in Arizona, and could have wished to have known fewer.

'Eh?' he enquired, in his turn. 'Yes, my good man, what is it?'

'Holliday?' pursued Seth, wanting to leave absolutely no room for the smallest doubt.

The Doctor considered the question. 'Well, yes – in a way, I suppose. Yes – you could say so...'

After all, he generally took a break at this time of year...

'Pleased to make your acquaintance,' ingratiated Seth. 'My name's Harper – Seth Harper...'

The despised name threaded its way through the key-hole of the back room, and sidled into Holliday's ear like an earthworm. He approached the door.

Light dawned on the Doctor – or, at any rate, he thought it did.

'Oh, I see... yes, Mr Harper? I presume you have

brought me a message from my friends?'

'Kind of a message, sure . . .'

This was going to be easy as . . . What was that crack of Phin's again? Something about frogs? It was going to be as easy as that, anyway . . .

'They're a-waitin' for you in the saloon. An' also there's this: the boys an' me would like you to join us for a drink.'

'Well, I must say, that is extremely sociable of you. But I fear I never touch alcohol . . . except for purely medicinal purposes, of course,' he added, remembering his recent foul experience.

'Not what I heard, Doc – but play it your way. Be there in five – no, maybe ten minutes.' After all, they had to arrange the set-up. 'Else we'll come a-lookin'.'

He left the shop backward, with a relief tempered only by his forgetting about the step. And Holliday, who had heard the whole exchange, suddenly realised exactly how the Doctor could settle his account . . . He entered, smiling like a coyote that has just stumbled on a beef steak in Death Valley.

'Did you hear that?' asked the Doctor. 'A complete stranger has just invited me to join him and his friends for a drink! How *very* kind, to be sure!'

'Jest typical Western hospitality is all,' murmured Doc. 'Goes along with tumbleweed an' deer an' antelope playin' the fool an' such. Oh, you'll soon learn. But forgive me for sayin' so, friend; in my opinion, you ain't dressed entirely right for the kind of a get-together like you're goin' to . . .'

'I fail to see in what respect my clothes are unsuitable. In fact, they are almost identical to your own, I notice . . .'

'Ain't they just? But it ain't your clothes so much, as

that you do not appear to be wearing a gun. You see, round here,' he continued, before the Doctor could embark on a pacifist diatribe, 'it's kind of an insult *not* to wear one. And you surely do not wish to go around insulting folks, do you now?'

'Of course I don't – but regrettably I have no gun to wear.'

'Is that truly so? Well, in that case, friend, looks like you'll just have to borrow one of mine...'

And, with the lightning rapidity which had made his name such a popular epitaph, he produced a Colt .45, and extended it in the general direction of the Doctor. Who winced once – and then lowered his hands, as he realised it was being offered butt first.

'Oh, but my dear fellow,' he protested, 'I couldn't possibly accept...'

'Come on now,' insisted Doc. 'You'll notice it's got my name right there on the grip? So it won't get lost no-how – an' you can return it before you leave town. And, say, you'd better take this gun-belt, as well – 'cause you don't want to go wavin' such a weapon around, or folks'll likely get the wrong idea... or else you'll shoot yourself in the foot, or whatever... Go on, take it!'

And he slung the lethal arbitrator round the Doctor's reluctant waist.

'There – now you look real smart!'

The Doctor admired himself in the cracked mirror.

'Well, this is extremely civil of you, I must say! But please – you really must let me give you... Oh yes, by the way, there is also the matter of my account. How much do I owe you altogether?'

'There ain't no charge at all, friend; seeing as how you're my very first patient, consider it on the house! Maybe I'll get your tooth silver-mounted as a keepsake.

It's a real beauty!'

'Well,' said the Doctor, overwhelmed by this further evidence of Western hospitality, goodwill, and camaraderie, 'I really don't know how I can pay you back.'

'You'll find a way, friend – you'll find a way. And you will also find the welcoming committee right along the street there . . .'

So, with expressions of mutual esteem, they parted; and the Doctor strode off to keep his appointment with History – and to redecorate the annals of the Golden West, while he was about it . . .

10

A Little Night Music

Left alone, Doc Holliday wasted a certain amount of time congratulating himself on his masterly grasp of essentials, and his generally unprecedented ability to kill two buzzards with one rock. Not only had he avoided putting his foot in a bear-trap, but he was confident that the little woman would thank him for doing so. Furthermore, in less time than it takes a Gila monster to prove it's the only poisonous lizard in the world, the substitute Doc Holliday would be a very dead ringer indeed!

So then he could start trading under a new name, to general acclaim and flag-flapping. How about that for a bowl of sweet potatoes and corn-pone, he asked himself?

Anxious to claim Kate's very special brand of congratulations, he spring-heeled back to the bedroom; only to find that the fiancée who had previously lent such a high tone to the love-nest had now departed for points elsewhere! All that remained to remind him of her was a note pinned to the pillow with an ice-pick...

'Why, you ornery, spineless, down-wind skunk,' it began affectionately, 'what kind of a belly-crawlin', ham-hearted, low-down, white livered apology for a no-good pistol-packing, knife-fighting, dental practising prairie-dog do you think you are, huh?

'Furthermore, how dare you let that nice old gentleman, who treated me with every courtesy, as if I was almost a lady – which is more than some do, let me tell you for nothing – where was I? – yes, how dare you let him go to front for you in a well-deserved show-down, and shortly occupy your reserved, unconsecrated parking-lot on Boot Hill? Answer me that!

'Well, at any rate, one of us has guts enough to wrap around the weekend whisky; and for your information I am goin' blazing down to the saloon right now to do what's right, while there's still time, and while the mood lasts!

'I have left a stew on the stove, which kindly do not allow to burn, as you will shortly do in hell, if there's any justice, which I doubt!

'More in sorrow than in anything else I care to name,
      'I am always,
      'Your previously loving,
      'Kate Elder, Miss, and likely to remain so!'

Holliday rubbed his chin – which didn't help any. Obviously, he considered, she had penned the document in something of a hurry, which would account for the somewhat erratic imagery; but still, reading between the lines, he could detect a bum's rush when he saw one. And he didn't like it. Wasn't he in the process of straining the honourable habits of a lifetime to make an honest fallen woman of her? Would he have sent an innocent man to his death if it hadn't been for the ennobling power of love? Not for a Royal Flush in Spades, he wouldn't! Well, maybe that was pushing it some, but nonetheless . . .

Well, you never knew with females, that was for sure! Always have to meddle with what don't rightly concern 'em, don't they? Still an' all, *when* they do, a man gotta likewise do what a man gotta do.

So, sighing like a distillery, he strapped on his second best gun-belt, tucked a Derringer into his boot, slung a Bowie knife round his neck, and thus loaded for bear, Childe Roland set out for the Dark Tower...

Meanwhile, at the Last Chance Saloon, the stage was already set – as if by an incompetent director. For the last half hour, Miss Dodo Dupont, piano, and Mr Steven Regret, heavy baritone, summoned from their rooms not so much by the lure of the bright lights as by Phin's buffalo gun, had been entertaining the gathering to a random selection of the songs you'd rather whistle; and everyone was getting a mite tired of it. The audience, in fact, was restive.

Well, to be fair, it ain't that easy to concentrate on the cabaret when you are at one and the same time watching the door for the Big Entrance of the fastest man who ever shot your brother. But, do them justice now, the Clantons were making a very brave effort.

Seth, on the other hand, wasn't. He was telling Charlie about how he had gone straight up to Holliday, bold as you please, and told him straight to his face how it would be if'n he didn't get his carcass down here where the fun was at, right soon...

'So why ain't he here?' asked the cynical bar-keep.

'Well, maybe I scared him some, at that,' admitted Seth, laughing down from lazy nostrils. 'Could be he's trying to get his dander up.'

Charlie thought this unlikely; but didn't like to say so

in the present company.

'Sure you got the right man?' he enquired. 'Lots of strangers in town fer the hangin'...'

'Which hangin'?' asked Seth, apprehensively.

'Whichever,' said Charlie. 'It's the time of year fer it...'

Whereafter the conversation flagged some.

In point of fact, the *wrong* man was even now trying to talk himself out of a misunderstanding at Ma Golightly's Place; where he had incautiously enquired if this was where his young friends were waiting. Well, they certainly were – but not the kind he wanted; and Ma, unused to complaints, had taken a certain amount of umbrage in consequence. And these things take time.

So, when the Big Entrance was made, it was Kate who made it – carrying a brace of pearl-handled shoot-me-downs Doc had given her as an engagement present. She figured she could return them later, along with the ring.

'Well, well, well!' she began, blasting the chandelier with a broadside. 'So Charlie's got hisself a new Burly-Q Queen, jest 'cause I turn my back for five minutes? Move it, sister – and I mean fast!'

'Bang!' she went again, so's Dodo would get the point. Which she certainly did, of course, quick as anything; but was in something of a quandary. I mean, here she and Steven were performing by urgent request of an armed audience; and here was Little Orphan Annie Oakley, or someone, suggesting, equally forcibly, that they desist.

So she paused in mid-arpeggio – that difficult bit, in the middle of 'Love, could I only tell thee...' it was; you probably know it – and glanced round to try and gauge the feeling of the majority.

But the majority was equally disconcerted.

It looks bad to let a dame get the drop on you; especially when you're the toughest bunch of no-account hombres as ever missed a spitoon; and for the moment they were uncertain how to proceed.

They looked to Ike for guidance; and he presently obliged with 'Best do as she says, little lady, if'n you want to grow old graceful. Kate's a mean one to get the wrong side of.'

Always difficult to say which was the wrong side of Kate Elder. Her every elevation was equally formidable, and Dodo wanted none of them.

'Very well,' she pouted. 'If that's your attitude, I'm sure I wouldn't wish to share the billing with an amateur!'

Not bad, really, on the spur of the moment; if a trifle unwise.

'Come, Steven,' she continued, 'let us return to our dressing-rooms – until such time as the management extends an apology!' And she looked enquiringly at Charlie, who *was* an apology, of course, but didn't care to extend himself just at the moment.

So up the stairs she flounced: and Steven was about to follow her with a more masculine version of the same exit, when Kate gave tongue once more.

'The feller stays here,' she said. 'I've been plannin' to get myself a new partner, an' looks like he's drawn the short straw! I like the cut of his jib,' she explained, somewhat confusingly; and took his arm, in a way which suggested further favours to come.

'Oh, do you?' said Steven, who had not hitherto realised he had a jib to cut. 'Thank you.'

'Well, thank *you*, Steven – and goodnight!' said Dodo. 'Please don't mind me! Just you go ahead and enjoy yourself with your new friend. I shall go to my room, and ponder on perfidy!'

And she stalked off to do both.

'Now then,' said Kate, 'seein' how everything's been arranged so amicable, let's you an' me show these boys how bar-room ballads from the Parlour Song Book should *really* be sung. Make with the piano, Mister!'

'Ah – now *there*, I'm afraid, you rather have me,' said Steven. '"Songs for all Occasions", possibly; but as far as the piano is concerned, all I know is "America the Brave".'

The ex-astronaut had, in fact, learned this as an essential part of his advanced course at Cape Canaveral, or someplace, and was rather proud of it.

'Then that's what we'll give 'em,' agreed Kate. 'Hats off boys – and the first one to hit a bum note in the chorus, gets it from me! O.K? A one, and a two...'

Since she was preparing to conduct the male voice choir with a revolver barrel, what could the boys do but clamber to their feet, remove their stetsons, and take a nervous breath – because the song, as you'll realise if you've ever tried it, isn't that easy.

So that is what they did.

And, with Steven Regret on the jangle-box, they were fairly launched into 'O, say can you see, by the dawn's early light' – which, in fact, they couldn't often – with Kate's cracked contralto soaring like a vulture over the toute ensemble, when the Doctor at last entered the bar.

11

And Some Durn Tootin'

On leaving his surgery, Doc Holliday – master of tactics as we have seen him to be – had decided, after tossing the idea around some, not to enter the saloon by kicking open the swing-doors, which could sometimes swing back and do you an injury; but to approach the premises from the rear, thereby preserving, he hoped, the highly spoken of element of surprise. For without some such, he was up against a stacked deck, whatever that may be; and he knew it.

So to this end, he made his pussy-footing way down Crum's Alley, scene of the late mayor's last reception; and with some thought for the probable effect on his gambler's finery, discarded the obvious plan of climbing a drain-pipe to the first floor of the Last Chance, in favour of the nimble leap from the back of an astonished horse to the rail of a sort of balcony affair; where he hung by his sensitive hands for a spell, reflecting on Life, Art, and what he would say to Kate when he found her again.

You will probably have seen this sort of manoeuvre executed countless times. But I'm here to tell you it ain't a peacherino by no means – especially without a standin who is paid to do it for you. And so, as I say, he took a brief pause for heavy breathing, and things of that nature.

But at last he managed to swing a leg or so over the balustrade; when, after a further pause to take a quick slurp from his hip-flask, he crashed spectacularly through the window of Dodo's bedroom. Where, as we know, she had gone to ponder on perfidy; and this new occurrence didn't help any! In fact, being a well-brought up girl, she was about to go so far as to scream the place down, when the Doc clapped a gloved hand over the in-breath.

Always wore gloves, these sort of characters – don't know why...

'Hush, little lady!' he advised; 'I'm a friend.'

She inspected his forbidding features as carefully as possible under the circumstances; and couldn't, for the life of her, remember them.

'Are you sure?' she enquired, as soon as her mouth was once more available. 'Perhaps you'd care to remind me of when and where?'

'Hush!' he counselled yet again. 'My name's Doc Holliday!'

Whereupon, having heard all about him and his widely reported unsavoury ways, she fainted.

Well, such things happen – and having urgent business of his own to attend to, Doc, with a muttered imprecation bearing on the generally unreliable nature of women, stepped over her heaving form, and emerged onto the landing; where he was just in time to witness the arrival of his understudy in the bar-room below.

'One more time, boys,' Kate was saying. 'We'll take it

from the top – an' try to remember that, for a red-blooded American, this song's kinda holy! So let's have a little damn reverence, shall we?'

But the Doctor, who had by now reached the bar unnoticed, was already applauding.

'Not at all,' he said. 'In my opinion that was an admirable rendition! Very well played, Steven, my boy! And I must say, Miss Elder, that for a dentist's receptionist, you sing most attractively. Bravo! What a stirring tune, to be sure!'

The boys were duly stirred, and wheeled rapidly on their heels to prove it. And to say they were also disconcerted is to put it mildly. I mean, it's one thing to gun a man down when he's negotiating a swing-door, and his hands are busy about it; but it's quite another to find him with his back against the bar, a monographed, low-slung six-gun, as they noticed, available for action, and when your own hands are occupied in clutching your head-gear over your patriotic heart. Where it wouldn't afford a deal of protection, when it came to the call!

No, sir! This needed thought. Especially as Steven and Kate were now behind *them*... Well, the best laid schemes, as they say...

Seth was the first to speak. Because it was he, after all, who had set up the arrangement, and he was duly proud of himself.

'Boys,' he said, with the air of a conjuror producing a horned toad from his hat; 'I'd like for you to meet the great Doc!'

'Thanks,' they muttered, grimly. They were going to take this up with him later...

The Doctor demurred. 'Oh, you flatter me there, I'm afraid. Reasonably accomplished, perhaps, but hardly "great". No, I can't allow that at all! Now, I believe, Mr Harper, that you were so kind as to invite me for a drink? And I must say, that after my recent experience, I would be extremely grateful for a glass of milk...'

This had the obvious effect of making them mistrust their ears. They were thrown, as the saying is, like steers in a stew-pond!

'Whatever's your pleasure, Doc,' said Charlie, affably – but wondering where in hell he'd find a glass of milk at this time of night. The cat, perhaps, might be of assistance in the matter. He went hurriedly to find out.

'What we really want, Doc, is a little talk,' interjected Ike, recapturing the initiative with some difficulty. 'A little talk about our brother, Reuben,' he explained further.

'Dear me! Is he in some sort of trouble?'

'You could say that,' agreed Phineas.

'On account he's dead,' contributed Billy. 'Dead as a coffin nail in a gallows-tree!'

'Well, I am extremely distressed to hear it,' sympathised the Doctor. 'What can I say? At a time like this, it is sometimes difficult to find the right words...'

'No, it ain't!' contradicted Ike, rudely. 'Not if a man's prepared to crawl, and say as he's truly sorry...'

'I believe I've already said so? But as to crawling... Oh, dear me, no! I can only venture to add, that perhaps his name will continue to live?'

'Surely will,' breathed Ike, 'on account it's Clanton!'

'We're the Clanton boys,' explained Phineas, justifying their interest.

'Oh dear!' said the Doctor.

'So you got it straight now?' asked Seth.

'You've heard of us, maybe?' asked Billy.

'Oh, indeed I have,' admitted the Doctor. 'And of

course of your father, the popular mayoral candidate. Yes, you are extremely well known... Ahem! Steven, my boy, I really think we should be going...'

Steven was the first to agree. But, on the other hand...

'But you ain't even drunk your nice milk yet,' Ike pointed out. 'An' Charlie's put himself out to go an' find some. Now, that ain't friendly... Also, it is inconsiderate!'

'Nevertheless, I can only suggest that you put the matter of your brother's untimely decease in the hands of the proper authorities. I fail to see how I can assist you...'

'You mean, like your friend, Wyatt Earp?' said Ike, nastily. 'Yes, I bet you'd like that jest fine!'

'Oh, I'd hardly say he was a friend – just a casual acquaintance, you know.'

'That ain't the way I heard it,' said Billy.

'Nor me neither,' said Phineas. 'The way we heard it, you an' him's closer than... than fleas on a hound-dog.' He grinned round for approval. Another good one!

'Wyatt Earp an' Doc Holliday,' sneered Billy. 'The bible-punchin' law-man, an' the drunken, good-fernothin' gambler! Now, ain't that somethin'?'

'Steady, boy,' cautioned Ike; 'let Seth handle it, like we arranged.'

Seth looked at them, plaintively. This wasn't like they'd arranged at all...

But the Doctor had seen the light – and about damn' time, too!

'Now, wait a moment,' he said. 'I think I begin to realise your mistake...'

'It's *your* mistake Seth's thinkin' of,' said Ike.

No, it wasn't. Seth was thinking something entirely

68

different; like, how in hell he'd got himself buffaloed into this in the first place.

'But I am not Doc Holliday! No – goodness me! – the man you wish to interview is the local dentist! You'll find him in his shop; and I am confident he will give you an appointment, if you approach him in a civil manner . . .'

'That's *where* I found you, ain't it?' grumbled Seth. 'And if that ain't enough, I declare, your name's right there on your gun-butt – so don't give us no argument!'

'But Holliday *lent* me this gun! Look here . . .'

And incautiously he drew the weapon, to show them. You shouldn't do a thing like that. Not in the West.

Well now, the Clantons *couldn't* draw, of course, because Kate was behind them, and *she* already had. And Steven was at least wondering *whether* to draw. But Seth, seeing no way out compatible with honour – which he'd heard about, some place – *did* draw . . . And a shot rang out, in that staccato way they have! And Seth's gun rocketed from his fist, spinning across the room to a well-earned rest in a cobwebbed corner, by the eventual-grill . . .

For a moment nobody moved – and it ain't hardly surprising! Because *Kate* hadn't fired; and Steven *thought* he hadn't; and the Clantons *knew* they hadn't.

But you, if you have been following closely, will realise that the bullet came by couresty of Doc Holliday – concealed, you may remember, on the landing.

However, the rest of the assembly did not have your advantages; and so assumed that the Doctor was responsible – well, the light was bad, Kate having damaged, you'll recall, the chandelier – and he didn't at once disillusion them. He was nobody's fool, after all . . .

'Why,' admired Phineas, 'I never even saw his hand

move!'

'He never even aimed!' complained Seth.

'My God, that was fast!' agreed the rest. 'We never did see nothin' faster! Wow!' they added.

'Well, let that be a lesson to you,' said the Doctor. 'Steven, my boy, – and you, Miss Elder, if you will be so kind – collect their fire-arms, and remove them to a place of safety. Out of their reach,' he elaborated.

Impressed, they hastened to obey.

'What do I do now?' he enquired of Kate, not being familiar with the protocol.

'You back 'em against the wall with their hands up,' she advised.

And so that's what he did.

But what he would have done next we shall never know; because, as Doc Holliday, with an air of business being temporarily adjourned, snaked his way back to Dodo's quarters, Wyatt Earp and Bat Masterson stomped into the action-packed water-hole.

12

Arrest Is As Good As A Change

'Howdy, Sinners! Holdin' a prayer-meetin'?' asked Wyatt. He could perhaps be forgiven for thinking so, in the atmosphere of awe-struck reverence which prevailed.

Bat said nothing. He generally left that kind of crack to his friend.

And the Doctor breathed the sigh of relief he'd been hoping to be able to use whenever convenient. 'Ah, my good Marshal!' he exclaimed. 'How very pleasant to see you! I was just trying to explain to these gentlemen...'

'It surely looks like you was explainin' – jest like Samson explainin' to the Philistines,' agreed Wyatt. 'But that ain't no jaw-bone of a mule you got there! So I suggest you hand it over – before the Temple of the Ungodly falls about your damn fool ears!'

'You too, Kate,' said Bat. 'Wyatt an' I handle that kind of explainin' round here!'

They obliged with various degrees of reluctance: and, not wishing to be left out of things, Steven added his own guns for good measure. He'd had enough of them for the time being.

'Now then,' said Wyatt, 'who started what?'

'Holliday did,' obliged Seth. 'He started the whole blame thing!'

Since Holliday wasn't noticeably present, this was something of a puzzlement.

'Holliday?' the lawmen enquired slowly, and in unison. They weren't here to be made fools of.

'Sure,' said Billy, 'we was jest havin' us a friendly sing-song...'

'Yeah,' said Ike, 'like cattle-men do round a camp fire, come nightfall. An' before we knew it, he got us lined up against the wall here... Look, ain't we against the wall?'

This was undeniable, but still...

'He was goin' to shoot us down in cold blood... like varmints in a... in a...'

'Shut up, Phin!' said Ike. 'Leave it at cold blood.'

'Cold as it comes,' agreed Billy. 'I tell you, Marshal, I saw the whole thing! I mean, I was *in* it, wasn't I?'

'An' so was I,' contributed Kate. 'An' the Doc got the drop on 'em fair an' square – accordin' to the rules laid down by Queensberry, or some feller. Seems like they was a-gunnin' for him.'

'Who isn't?' said Bat, scratching his singed moustache. 'But that still don't explain...'

'Quiet, Bat!' warned Wyatt, looking like the prophet Jeremiah after a bad morning.

Behind the Marshal's marble brow, there moved a mind of ice-like acumen; and in rather more time than it takes to tell, he had weighed the situation in the balance; and found it short on equilibrium. But that didn't mean he was unable to work out that what he had here was a case of mistaken identity. And he thought that, all things considered, it would be best to leave it that way, for the time being.

'Guess it all seems pretty clear,' he agreed. 'I'm sorry, Doc, but I've got to take you in.'

'I am not taken in for a moment!' contradicted the Doctor. 'This whole situation is a...' What was the expression he wanted? 'A frame-up!' he remembered, 'that's what it is!'

'Be that as it usually be,' continued the imperturbable monument, 'you're under arrest!'

'Arrest? How *dare* you? May I remind you that this is the second time today you have forced me to ask that? And you have absolutely no excuse for this constant custody! You know perfectly well who I am!'

'Surely do, old friend,' agreed Wyatt, 'which is why I aim to put you out of harm's way for a spell.'

'Then I demand to see a solicitor!'

'You wouldn't take to him,' said Phineas, 'not no-how! Why, he's bent as a craw-dad's claw in a swamp-hole!'

'I've warned you, Phin,' hissed Ike. 'Let it lay, cain't you?'

Phineas subsided, muttering resentfully, and the Doctor, also muttering, and with my Buntline Special hard against his ribs, was prodded towards the door; with Bat on shot-gun at coverpoint.

'Goodnight, sinners!' said Wyatt to the congregation; 'I'm sorry your stay in this festering haunt of the Malachite has been so rudely disturbed...'

And the three men backed warily into the West-infested darkness...

Left to themselves, the rest of the company was something at a loss for words, and groped for them accordingly.

Kate was the first to find some, and spoke as follows: 'Well now, gentlemen, if that concludes the evening's entertainment, and you don't want no quick gallop through "The Star-Spangled Banner", I guess I'll be goin' back to my room... An' that's where I'll be if anyone wants me,' she added, with a glance from beneath her half-mast lashes at Steven, who chose to ignore her, having quite enough to panic over at the moment, without any of *that* nonsense... And, disappointed, Kate oscillated up the stairs.

'Well, if that don't beat all,' said Phineas, referring not to her retreating silhouette, which left nothing to the imagination, but to the recent events, which did.

'It figures,' said Ike, as near to thoughtfully as he would ever get. 'Earp couldn't take us in for nothin', so he got the Doc out of trouble, like always.'

'He weren't in no trouble,' objected Billy. 'He made Seth look right foolish. You should've let me handle it, like I wanted!'

'Don't know so much about that,' said Seth. 'You boys didn't look a lot like the James gang, not from where I was standing. More like the Mariposa Glee Club,' he concluded.

'Well,' said Steven; 'if there's nothing else?'

'Sit down!' said Ike.

'Right down!' added Phineas.

'Jest stay where you are!' said Billy, pursuing a line of his own, 'whiles I get us our hardware...'

Too late Steven remembered that their guns were now once more readily available...

Well you can't think of everything, can you?

Arriving back in her sewing-room, our smouldering

songstress was not best pleased to find it already occupied by the rival soubrette; and she was downright chagrined to hear the latter enquiring of Doc Holliday just how long he proposed to keep her there.

Kate was understandably more interested to learn just how long he had kept her there already, and enquired as much, with a wealth of illustrative detail intended to convey what would likely occur if his answer failed to satisfy her in any particular.

Dodo blushed, and Doc prevaricated.

'Why, Kate,' he admonished, 'you know me! Would I ever be a party to that kind of actionable misdemeanour?'

'You're durn tootin'!' commented his outraged inamorata, without a great deal of logic. She removed a boot, and prepared to press the heel into service as a stiletto. It was a large boot, as we have already noticed, and Doc looked apprehensive...

'Now, put that thing away, Kate, before it goes off! I was jest explainin' to the little lady here...'

'Seems to me there's been a sight too much goddam explainin' took place around here for one night! Know what you are, you ornery, crawlin' apology fer a ringtailed, downright rabid racoon?'

'I know; I know right well, Kate – I read your note. I have already registered your sentiments; an' that's why I come a-runnin'...'

'So's you could shack up with someone else, before sun-down caught you lonely? Didn't take you long, did it?'

'Kate, I came so's I could protect you from your illadvised an' head-strong ways! Know what them Clantons is likely to do to a defenceless woman?'

She didn't recognise the description.

'Seems to me like it was them as needed protectin'! I took care of the whole thing; whilst you was a-canoodlin' with your fancy piece of small-time, low-tone, high-falutin' jail-bait here! Makes me puke!' she added, to explain her attitude.

Dodo was about to object to this character summary with some heat, when Holliday forestalled her. He didn't want a war of the wild-cats on his hands, on top of everything else . . .

'So who was it took care of Seth Harper, then, since you're so all-fired smart?'

He let the question float in the air; where Kate gave it her grudging attention.

'That was you?'

'Not only a privilege, but a pleasure,' said Doc modestly. 'S'pose you was too busy conductin' the Ragtime Four to notice?'

'Then, for Pete's sake, why didn't you get him between the eyes, like a feller should?'

'Oh, come on, Kate – be fair! I mean, have you *seen* his eyes? There just ain't rightly room for a bullet between 'em. They kind of overlap,' he explained to Dodo. ''Sides, if I'd truly killed him, what would've happened to the old guy you're so dad-blasted fond of? He'd have been deader'n a prime hog came Thanks-givin'! The Clantons may be slow, but they're accurate . . .'

'Which old guy?' asked Dodo, who had been out of the swim of events for some time.

'Why, Honey,' said the somewhat ameliorated Kate, 'a real nice old guy, who came in to get a tooth fixed.'

Dodo blanched. 'But that must have been my friend, the Doctor!' she deduced. 'Why would they want to kill *him*?'

'On account they took him fer Sir Galahad over there,' explained Kate, nodding towards Holliday with her bosom, 'who had the kindness to set him up for it, the bastard!' she added.

'Then where is he now? I must go to him!'

'I'd not advise it, Sugar,' said Kate, her heart of brass now more or less won over, 'seein' as how Wyatt Earp's jest got through arrestin' him.'

'Arrested? But what on earth for?'

''Cause Wyatt didn't see fit to disabuse 'em of the notion that he was Holliday.'

'But why?'

'God knows, Molasses,' Kate admitted, 'but I'd say it was a fair bet that, like always, he was lookin' out for his fine friend, here. Kind of drawin' the Clantons' fire.'

'Onto the Doctor? But that's awful!'

'Now don't you go worryin' none, little lady,' interjected Holliday. 'If he's with Wyatt, he couldn't be no safer. Only man as I ever respected,' he explained.

Now that was a strange friendship: born of favours more or less accidentally received in the course of mayhem and general carnage, he supposed. But there it was. And, oddly, though they were, as you might say, on the opposite sides of the law, it had lasted through a score of cow-towns they had tamed together.

So now . . . 'What do you ladies say to a little three-handed game of chance?' he enquired.

After all, he didn't want to waste the entire evening . . .

13

The Red Hand of Tradition

Meanwhile, the Doctor, still spluttering with inexorable indignation at his captors, was having it firmly and forcibly explained to him that if he so much as put his interfering snout outside the gaol-house before Holliday could be persuaded to leave town – when the matter of mistaken identity could safely be resolved to universal rejoicing and jocular back-slapping – then, certain as a possum goes with cold potatoes, he would get it shot from his fool face by four of the toughest characters as ever put pincer to toe-nail.

'Don't mistake the Clantons none,' warned Bat. 'Just because, for some cock-a-mamie reason, you got away with it the once! O.K. – maybe they're a mite sponge-witted an' slow-spoken to your way of thinkin', but that don't decelerate 'em none when it comes to back-shootin' an' side-swipin' an' such! An' fer another thing, they got Seth with 'em – an' he's about the slimiest crittur ever got trod by human foot!'

This was a long speech for Bat, and he appealed to Wyatt to continue the argument . . .

'Main thing is though,' said Jehovah's sidekick, 'that they got their Pa behind 'em – which is a situation that

78

personally I would never seek. Because the said Pa Clanton is jest about the nastiest *pater familias* a growin' boy could go in holy terror of! An' he ain't about to relish this laughable little set-back, but no-how. Now, his business with Doc Holliday is kind of a private matter concernin' the premature demise of his eldest. But his business with me is that I claim the God-given right to stop him takin' over the whole county for his personal purposes – which are downright unpleasant!'

'Rustlin',' said Bat.

The Doctor listened – but couldn't hear anything himself, so relaxed again.

'An' horse thievin', an' stage hold-ups, an' bullion robbery,' continued Bat; 'an' they do say,' he lowered his voice, 'that he's defrauded the tax-office a time or two . . .'

'Too many slap-happy returns,' confirmed Wyatt, 'an' him standin' for mayor, an' all!'

'As well as murder, an' all,' continued Bat.

'And all? And all what?' asked the Doctor.

'The feller drinks!' said Wyatt.

'Well now, Wyatt, so does Holliday,' objected Bat. 'You got to admit that . . .'

'That's different,' said Wyatt. 'He's my friend.'

And he set to cleaning his revolver with a consecrated oil-rag . . .

And simultaneously with this succinct exposition of the *casus belli*, the boys in the bar-room were busy scaring the hell out of that disenchanted dude, Jazz-fingers Steven Regret, late of the intergalactic force for good, and dedicated to fighting evil in all its forms.

The trouble was, he hadn't encountered it in *this* form

before; not combined with what seemed to him to be boneheaded, crass stupidity!

'For God's sake!' he exploded at length. 'Why can't you listen? For the last time, I tell you that man is *not* Doc Holliday! I don't care *what* Earp said – he's nothing like him! I don't suppose,' he added, not being entirely sure on that point.

'He sure enough shoots like him,' said Seth, ruefully.

'Sure 'nough does!' agreed the others. 'Fast? We ain't never seen nothin' like it! We said so at the time, if you remember?'

'But *he* didn't fire that shot! He probably wouldn't know how.'

'Haw! Haw!' they went, with subtle sarcasm – rather like a rookery in the Springtime.

'In any case, the bullet came from upstairs – I was watching!'

'Well, Glory be!' admired Phineas. 'He got eyes like a bald eagle, this feller! He can watch bullets come an' go like they was flappin' their wings!'

This was his best yet; and there was a short pause for refreshment, while they congratulated him.

'Never mind all that,' said Steven, irritably. 'You'll simply have to take my word for it.'

They fell about some more.

'Because what I've got to do now is get him out of gaol ...'

'Stop it!' they begged. 'Oh, please – no!'

And they wiped their streaming noses on the table-cloth.

'I don't see what's so funny – the Marshal had absolutely no right to arrest him!'

'So what you're goin' fer to do, I take it,' said Ike, when he felt better, 'is you're ... oh, dear ... you're gonna walk right down into that there abode of the righteous, gun down Earp and Masterson . . . an' then you an' your friend, who ain't by no means Doc Holliday, is jest gonna ride your sweet way outa town? Is that it?'

'Well, no – not exactly,' Steven admitted. 'No, I shall reason with them. I mean, they're both intelligent men – they're bound to see there's just been a misunderstanding . . . I should think . . .'

'Boys,' said Ike, 'seems to me like our young pal here could use a little help.'

'Sure could,' the rest agreed.

'You see, Mr Regret,' continued Ike, 'to *my* way of thinkin', it looks like we all got us the same problem: namely, how to restore your partner to the fresh, pure air of liberty . . .'

'That's right,' Phineas agreed. 'So's we can blast the livin' day . . .'

'Shut up, Phin! So's we can have a little talk, an' find out who he *really* is. Because, if he really *ain't* the Doc, like you say . . . well, we wouldn't want to see no miscarriage of justice, would we, boys?'

Here he winked laboriously at all brothers within eyeshot.

'Certainly wouldn't,' they assured him. 'That would be too damn' bad!'

'So we got to think us of a plan.'

'I've been trying to,' said Steven.

'Then you can lay off right now – 'cause I just thought me of a dilly! It's simple, it's effective; and furthermore, it's traditional! You boys know what I'm talkin' about?'

They didn't.

'Well then, look-ee here: all we gotta do is get us a rope.'

They liked that.

'Then we tie it round the neck of Mr Regret, here; an' we lead him, like he was a hound-dog, to the hangin'-tree in front of the gaol-house. So then, if his friend *don't* come out, to take his place . . .'

'What?' gulped Steven.

'Why then, we're simply goin' to have to pretend to lynch you . . .'

'Pretend?'

'Why sure; unless somethin' happens to get us riled – like maybe, Wyatt an' Bat tearin' into us with shot-guns, or some such . . . but no – they'd never do that, with you standin' right there in front of us, would they now?'

'Suppose they do?'

'Well then,' said Ike, reasonably, 'in that far-fetched eventuality, we'd jest have to review the situation some. Play it by ear,' he explained, 'where the knot'll be . . .'

He sat back; like Napoleon rolling up the map of Europe. Yes, he was pleased with his plan.

'Reckon it'll work?' demanded Billy.

'Why, boy, don't you ever read nothin' bar Wells Fargo catalogues? Of course it'll work. It always works. A man has to come out to save his friend, don't he? Irrespective of any small, personal risk? I tell you, it's traditional! So what do you all say?'

By a majority of four to one, Charlie abstaining, the motion was carried; and, mumbling something about frogs, Phineas lumbered off to find them a hempen neck-tie.

14

The Law and Doc Holliday

Upstairs, there was something of a strained atmosphere, as Dodo counted her winnings – or raked them towards her, like they say. She had learned all about poker at her finishing school; and the lessons had included a few modern refinements unknown to Doc Holliday, who was sore as a bear in a bee-tree in consequence.

'Tarnation blazes!' he snarled, having rejected his first choice of exclamation out of deference to the all-female company. 'Ma'am, it would ill behove me to accuse a well-brought-up little lady, like your sweet self, of concealin' wildies in her unmentionables, but ...'

'Then don't!' said Dodo. 'Put up, or shut up! Want some more?'

'Lady, I *got* no more! You jest cleaned me out! Reckon I'll have to step down to the bar for a spell, and replenish my resources from the pockets of the sportin' fraternity ...'

'You stay where you are, Doc Holliday!' said his beloved Kate, snapping like an angry garter. 'The Clanton boys'll likely still be infestin' the place, an' you promised me you'd stay out o' trouble!'

'Well now, you see, Kate, I also do have this dryness

creepin' up from my throat, an' . . .'

'Sit down! Less'n you give some spry sign of reformation, it's all over between us!'

'But I'd kind of calculated from your fratchetty manner as it *was* all over. An' now you're sayin', unless I truly go to the Devil I cain't *ever* be rid of you? Aw, come on, Kate: you know I got no dearer wish than to do like you say – if only you'd say it gentle! All I hanker after from now on, is you cookin' an' me eatin' – you know that!'

Whereupon she softened somewhat; as women will, under the influence of such rosy-spoken tributes to their domestic know-how . . .

'Times you really do melt a gal's heart right down to gravy, you glib, smooth-talkin' thimble-rigger, you! Never did rightly know which to choose between you an' Turkey-Creek Johnson, till he got hisself hung,' she reflected. 'O.K. then, Sweet-talk, seein' you're that set on my victuals, did you take the stew off the stove, like I told you in my billet-doux?'

'Damn!' said Doc Holliday. And simultaneously remembering a bottle of rot-gut he'd secreted in the scalpel steriliser, he left the place by that same window wherein he came, and went to attend to it.

Following his nose, Doc readily traced the blackened repast to its ptomaine domain; and, having consigned the remains to a labour-saving crematory, he was about to rehydrate himself from the aforementioned germ-free bottle, when he was given pause by what felt like the mouth-piece of a cannon in the small of the back.

Now, who would do a thing like that – without first taking the obvious precaution of pulling the trigger, that is?

Only one man he knew would have the goddam nerve: and presently the gloomy, Revivalist tones of his assailant assured him that his supposition was correct . . .

'Howdy, old child of darkness an' sorrow,' purred Wyatt. 'Come to pass your time in confession to an old acquaintance?'

'Well now,' said Doc, 'I ain't much in the line of weepin' or wailin' these days, but with the gnashin' of dentures I can surely oblige. An' if'n you'll be so civil as to place that there weapon back in its leather receptacle, it'll be a real pleasure to see you, Wyatt. Mind if I turn up the lamp, so I can refresh myself with a glimpse of them time-worn features?'

The Marshal offered no objection; and as the smoky flame illuminated the tobacco-stained appointments of the dream kitchen, he was pleased to see Holliday remove the point of a Bowie knife from the region of his fourth weskit button; and the two friends took cautious stock of each other.

It had been a long time, and there'd be a heap to discuss between them. Wyatt began the discussion.

'I'd like it fine,' he said, 'if you was to get the hell out of town!'

'An' like hell I will!' said Doc pleasantly. 'Now, where'd I put that bottle? You'll join me, Wyatt?'

'Drink is an abomination to the Lord!' declined Wyatt.

'Wasn't invitin' Him, as I recall,' said Doc, 'but each to his own pizen, like they say. Now me, I can accomodate the occasional swig of abomination, without sufferin' greatly.' And he proceeded to prove it . . .

'Long as you're sober enough to ride,' pursued Wyatt, grimly.

'Now Marshal, when have you ever seen me drunk? The booze an' I came to an amicable understandin' some years gone: it don't never back up on me, so long as I never let up on it! No, let me advise you Wyatt; it's when you discontinue the lubrication that them crimson gophers part your scalp with a meat axe. Like they was jest doin',' he explained. 'So if you'll kindly excuse me, while I pacify 'em some . . .'

'Don't take all night about it, then; I mean what I say.'

Doc wiped his moustache with a surgical swab.

'Can you please explain to me, Wyatt, why every son of the morning I meet gives me that self-same message? Bat Masterson, now – he started in on it before I'd fairly got here. An' I've done nothin' agin the law – well, not recent,' he qualified.

'Bat wants you out 'cause he don't like you: with me, it's 'cause I do. Comes to the same thing though, don't it? So you'd best git!'

'For pity's sake, why? I jest opened this here much-needed clinic. An' moreover, I aim to get married right soon; to a real fine . . . well, to a real woman, anyway!'

'A Jezebel of Babylon,' commented Earp.

'No, a Kate Elder of Sourdust Creek,' corrected Doc. 'You probably know her. Most people do,' he remembered, gloomily. 'Big girl in boots.'

'I seen her around some,' confessed Wyatt. 'Had the pleasure of removin' her gun-belt only this evening.'

'That strikes me as bein' a mite familiar, when she's an engaged party . . .'

'An' I've no objection to your takin' her along with you, if such be your hell-bent inclination. But this thing's your own fault, Doc: seemingly you set up this here other Doctor for a headstone he somehow side-stepped; an' I cain't keep him in the gaol-house forever; not till Judgement Day neither, whichever be the sooner. An' when I *do* let him loose, there's gonna be questions. Which questions, when answered, will likely prove he ain't you. So by then, you'd best be long gone; else there'll be gun-play in the streets'll make the Alamo look like ... like the Boston Tea Party,' he concluded, lamely.

'Now, come on Wyatt – you know you an' me – an' maybe Bat, if'n he'll tolerate my company – you know we can take care of the Clantons, for sweet sake!'

'*And* the McLowries; an' any other law-shy gunsel Pa Clanton chooses to throw at us? No, Doc – before *that* kind of Armageddon is declared, I got to have my brothers to back me. I already sent for 'em – but Virgil an' Warren's got a way to come; an' Morgan – well, he ain't no more than a boy. Now, if you're around *before* they get here, Doc, there'll be no holdin' the outbreak of hostilities. So I ain't askin' you to go forever, understand? Just until the hosts of the Righteous is well-assembled. Then maybe I'll send for you – so stay close, so's I can get word ...'

'Well, thank you kindly, an' here endeth the first lesson,' bowed Doc. 'I don't like it, Wyatt; it don't come at all natural to run!'

'I'm not askin' you to like it – I'm *tellin'* you to go! An' furthermore, if you ain't gone come sun-up, then I greatly fear, friend, that Bat an' I'll have to ...'

'I know, I know – you'll come a-lookin'! Ain't it always the same?' he grumbled, for the second time that day.

Then, tucking the bottle under his arm, he turned his offended back on the flail of the Lord, and sashayed back to base.

15

A Very Nasty Little Incident

You may have wondered, during the course of this brief history, why a popular sink of iniquity, such as the Last Chance, remained so singularly free of paying customers during licensed hours? And the answer is simple: word had got around that the Clantons were whooping up the place, that's why. And that's all.

So, for the best part of a whole day, the thirst-racked walk-on parts had been prowling the town, looking for alternative distractions. Ma Golightly, for one, had done very well out of it; and at the Bird Cage Theatre Eddie Foy was thinking that if business went on like this, they were going to hit Broadway with a box-office bonanza which could only be described as a smackeroo! On such imponderables does showbiz depend . . .

But by now, Main Street was beginning to fill with a rebarbative rabble of recidivists who wanted to know what in hell was going on in there so's a man couldn't get a drink when he was all tuckered out, playin' guitars, an' such . . . ?

And this was the tinder, apt for a demagogue's match, which the Clantons found assembled, as they finally emerged to promote their already revealed plans for the

Doctor's discomforture.

Seth wasn't with them, no, sir! He was a gunfighter, wasn't he? And by no means about to become involved in a vulgar lynching, calculated to attract the disapproval of Wyatt Earp. That's not what he was paid for, for God's sake!

But Steven unavoidably *was* present; and Ike now dragged him forwards, and presented him to the ready-made audience for their consideration.

'You know what we got here, friends?' he enquired.

They didn't at once, no. And they cared less. Some dude, they supposed, bound for the high jump – and probably serve the feller right, at that! But what they wanted right now was a drink, thank you; so, if the Clantons wouldn't mind stepping aside, they would be grateful!

But Ike was not the man to let a matter drop, once he'd got fairly started.

'This here sneering son of Satan is a friend of Doc Holliday's,' he persevered, 'the rat-featured dentist in whose presence no decent tooth is safe in its bed. And who, furthermore, killed our brother,' he remembered, having been prompted by Phineas.

'Well now, since the aforementioned is currently cowering in custody behind the guns of your bent sheriff, and his crony, the sanctimonious Earp, what we propose to do is this: we – that is, my remaining brothers and I – are going to stretch this feller's neck a little; to see if that won't make Holliday come out an' face us in a law-abidin' manner, instead of cowering cravenly in custody behind the guns of your bent . . .

'You already said that . . .' counselled Billy.

'Well, anyway, you get the idea? So while we're a-doin' that, I suggest that you all express your outraged feelings by smashing into Holliday's sadistic emporium, and availing yourselves of its valuable contents; which he won't likely be needin' no more . . .'

'Once we've finished with him that is . . .' contributed Phineas.

'They know that, Phin – they *know* that! God's sake, they ain't plumb stupid!'

Of course they weren't – well, not completely plumb.

One of them presently raised the shout of 'Sure!' and the cry was soon taken up. So while Steven was rope-hauled, hog-tied along Main Street to his fatal appointment, the extras lit torches – for some reason – and then swirled angrily in and out of the toothery; bearing off such items as bone-forceps, scalpels, probes, and – once they got around to it – that pride of Doc's life, the late death-chair from San Quentin.

That would teach him wouldn't it?

Sure! Sure!

It is never easy to explain to a girl who has recently been the recipient of your heart-held promise to settle down and set your slippers out to smoulder, that, on the other hand, you are about to leave town for an indefinite period. The apparent contradiction tends to attract criticism; and Doc Holliday was finding that no exception had been made in his case.

Kate was as mad as a hornet in a trombone; and having used up most of her picturesque phraseology on the clarification of his other inadequacies, she was now resorting to the violence of which she was so well-known a practitioner.

'But Honey,' said Doc, removing the remains of a giant economy size pot of face-cream from his previously immaculate lapels; 'you know I'd ride through hell an' back for you! It's just that, on this occasion, I'd like for you to come with me. We'll both enjoy it – it'll be a break,' he added, without much conviction.

'You think so, do you?' she enquired, reaching for a handsome bronze statuette of the Venus de Milo with an egg-timer in its stomach, which had been an admired appurtenance of her business premises in Acapulco. 'Take that!'

'Now Kate, what could I possibly do with such a provocative gew-gaw?' he objected, catching it in mid-flight, and returning it to stock. 'You know right well that if I don't leave town, Wyatt'll be gunnin' for me, come sun-up. And one thing I never done in my whole life is shoot the guts out of a friend. Always been a close-held principle of mine – although right now, you're stretchin' it some,' he admitted.

'Oh, he's a real gentleman, ain't he, Sugar?' she appealed to Dodo, now resorting to tears – which, she had been told, could often be effective at such times . . .

She had been misinformed. The effect was similar to that of a hot-spring erupting in a mud-hole; and Holliday, not wishing her to make a filthy habit of the manoeuvre, said as much.

As for Dodo, she was, for once, uncertain as to *what* to say. If this was the widely advertised Love, she thought, she would be quite content to leave it to the older generation for the foreseeable . . . Besides, she had no wish to intrude on such a private moment; and so, being a sensible girl, she changed the subject, before it became exhausted.

'Oh, look,' she said, 'they're lighting a bonfire in the street! Isn't that pretty?'

It may have been – but it was also Holliday's shop; and he registered the fact with an astonished and indignant snarl.

'By God, they've got my chair!' he exclaimed and leapt through the door, fire-arms springing from every holster and ticket-pocket en route.

Such of you as had been previously concerned by the lack of custom in the bar may have also added a footnote to the effect that it was about damn time we had a little action round here. After all, it's a Western, ain't it? Well, here it is at last, friends; and don't blame me if it's a bit on the bloody side!

You will possibly remember that, for reasons of his own, our hired gun-tuner, Seth Harper by name, had elected to remain in the saloon, rather than join the ensuing whoopee with the maddened mob outside. You do? Good.

Well, then – he was now quietly occupied in draining the sludge-like sediment from the greasy glasses left on the bar by his friends and colleagues; at the moment when inspiration had struck them, as with a branding-iron.

Not a *lot* in it for him, of course; but 'waste not want not' had ever been his monosyllabic watch-words – and why not, I ask you? A man got precious few perquisites at his end of the business, the golden rewards of effort going largely to his employers.

So he was thus engaged when Holliday hit the stairs like a dry-season twister, and began his meteoric descent of same. All still might have been well, and they could have passed like ships in a bottle, with no harm done; had not Dodo, who had been watching the ebb

and flow of events in Main Street from her bedroom
window, chosen that very moment to holler after the
retreating dentist, words to this effect: 'Doc, they've got
my friend Steven out there! Oh, please, please, save him
from the many-headed monster! Please, Doc!'

Well, that was the gist of it, anyway; but the point to
note is that she not only said 'Doc' but that she said it
twice!

The word sank into Seth's unpractised mind, like a
gleam of truth in a naughty world, as the saying is. And
he levered himself away from the bar, into the very path
of the cyclone. Of course, he'd been drinking heavily for
some years, else he'd've never; but still, that's what lack
of temperance'll do for you sometimes. One moment,
you're on top of the cock-eyed world – and the next,
you're telling the muscle-man in the corner that if he
looks at you sideways again, you'll knock his head off!
That's the way it goes, in my experience.

And that's how it went with Seth. 'Back up there,
friend!' he said. 'Wait jest one little minute, will you?'

Strangely perhaps, Holliday obliged. Oh, he
recognised Seth, all right, but he fancied he was secure
in his own anonymity; and besides, he was, as we have
seen at all times, a gentleman; and it was his impression
that the gun-man was perhaps in need of a match, or
some such. He therefore raised a brow enquiringly,
while glancing at his fob-watch. 'Can maybe give you a
moment,' he agreed politely, 'but I'm in something of a
hurry.'

'Seems to me,' continued Seth, laboriously, 'that
some party jest addressed you as Doc?'

Expressing silent thanks to Dodo, Holliday confirmed that this was indeed the case.

'Well now, could it be that this high falutin'

soubriquet is but the prefix to the further word, "Holliday", by any chance?'

It was not in Doc's nature to deny the truth when it was unavoidable. So he agreed that the name had been attached to him in infancy, and had clung there ever since.

'In that case, friend, you ain't goin' no place – except maybe to hell!' Seth qualified.

Too late he remembered that, whereas he was now alone, Holliday had his reputation with him. But, oh, what the hell? He'd started the thing now, and couldn't rightly figure how to discontinue. So he reached for his gun . . .

His eyes, as we have previously noted, had always been close: but now they felt that something had come between them. They were right. Doc had performed a miracle of marksmanship, and squeezed a bullet into that tiny gap!

As he sank to his knees, Seth's last draining thought was that if he'd played things right in his youth, and studied hard, he could perhaps have been a school-teach . . . if only he hadn't been so god-damned ug . . . ly . . .

But that was it! No use thinking along those lines now – and he'd nothing left to do it with, anyway . . . Because the last drops of his inadequate brains were oozing bloodily on to his go-to-show-down weskit . . . So he subsided slowly to the sawdust, and left it at that.

Well, I warned you, it weren't by no means pretty.

94

16

Wyatt Plays It By The Book

Some moments later, Charlie, bar-proud entrepreneur that he was, mopped up Seth's slimy detritus with a face-flannel, and felt he'd better say something because he'd been warned about this sort of carry-on in his premises by Bat.

'Stranger,' he said judicially, 'you shouldn't rightly have done that...'

'So I'm supposed to stand back at three paces, till such time as he gets the range worked out? Look at this!' said Doc, indicating the splattered *corpus delicti*. 'Bits of him all over my boots! Borrow your flannel?'

'And welcome,' said Charlie, agreeably. After all, the late Mr Harper had not been a highly valued customer.

'So then, I'll be on my way – long as you don't plan to give me no further argufyin' – 'cause I don't take kindly to such...'

Having registered his complaint, Charlie assured him that, as far as he was concerned, the matter was now closed.

'But if'n you are indeed Doc Holliday,' he continued, 'which personally I am now prepared to believe, then if I was you, I wouldn't go out there. There's a mob fixin' to lynch you,' he explained.

'Now why in tarnation would they want to do an unfriendly thing like that? I mean, conflagratin' my surgery, an' stealin' my chair is one thing – two things,' he amended. 'But lynchin' is pushin' it some!'

'The Clantons has got 'em all riled up... an' supposin' they hadn't, you've jest given 'em another pretty fair excuse for a hang-me-high, I'd say. No offence, of course.' He reached for the bleach, and sprinkled it some. 'But you know how towns-folk is? One touch o' fancy shootin', an' they're sayin' it ain't safe fer their kids to step into a bar-room no more! No, if I was you, Mister, I'd have lit out backwards by now.'

So here was yet another deportation order, however friendly meant; and, for the first time, Doc began to wonder if there was maybe something in it, at that. Because you gotta be more than fast to get the drop on a whole town – you gotta be mayor; which he wasn't. And no use appealing to a higher authority for help, either; since the said authority had already hoofed him in the slats, and told him to get lost come sun-up! So what was one chair more or less, he finally figured.

Somewhere over the far-away hills would be a booze-packed, shining new horizon; and rolling summer meadows, no doubt, crammed with rotten teeth for a man to pick. So, what the hell?

Furthermore, considering Wyatt's unfriendly attitude, the latter could damn well whistle for assistance come Doomsday as far as he was concerned!

And he had just arrived at this gloomy conclusion when his female dependants joined him, descending the stairs as women do at such times, both hands on the same rail, and assorted expressions of frozen horror on their chalk-white features.

Actresses do quite a lot of this, of course; but even amateurs can usually manage an approximation, when pushed; which Dodo and Kate considered they had been.

'Are you responsible for that?' demanded Kate, pointing to Seth's mortal remains with a quivering, paste-bedizened forefinger.

'Not any more,' disclaimed Doc. 'Rightly speakin', he's the concern of the mortician, as of now. I just washed my boots of him...'

Interesting enough, naturally; but Dodo had other, more urgent matters in mind. 'Forget all that!' she said. 'Have you rescued Steven yet? Where is he?'

'Well now, I'll tell you how it is,' he said, slowly, 'if you'll both kindly discontinue your well-meant whining. As I see it, Miss Dodo, if your friend, Steven, is goin' to be extracted from his unfortunate predicament, then steadier and more numerous hands than mine are called for; which, ideally speaking, should be backed up by the full majesty of rough justice; such as can be more suitably administered by Wyatt an' Bat, whose responsibility such a recrudescence of blind blood lust rightly is.

'They're bound to notice what's goin' on, give 'em time; which time we are now goin' to utilise by gettin' the hell out of here; an' installin' ourselves for the nonce in a nearby hide-away I know of.

'So, Kate, you will now oblige me by bringin' the buggy to the rear entrance – as has been your helpful habit on previous and similar occasions. An' meanwhile, you, Miss Dodo, would help considerable if you would kindly button your flappin' lip!'

'But I must go to Steven and the Doctor!' wailed Dodo. 'They need me,' she explained.

'Cain't think *why* they would,' he said. 'Time he's facin' his last reckonin', a man don't relish the jabberin' o' females. Leastways, such has been my frequent experience – as I've often taken it on myself to inform Kate. So don't argue – *git!*'

And toying meaningfully with a gun-butt, he shepherded his bleating little flock out of that place; and pretty soon they were raising the dust, safely installed in a Surrey – but with no immediate prospect of a binge on top.

They were headed for that unpopular resort and salt-spring spa – Purgatory Bend.

Doc had been right about Wyatt and Bat: they noticed what was going on in practically no time at all – and invited the Doctor to come and enjoy the view from the gaol-house window.

'Now see what you've done?' said Wyatt. 'The Assyrians descend like the wolf on the fold!'

'Do they?' enquired the Doctor. 'Oh, my goodness, so they do! But I refuse to accept any responsibility; I have done nothing whatever to encourage them!'

''Cept maybe 'personate the meanest killer as ever made 'em look right foolish,' agreed Bat, 'an' that'll do it, every time.'

It was not, to be honest, a comfortable sight which advanced to claim their attention. The milling mob had squeezed the last drop of possible entertainment from the Holliday home, and was now swirling purposefully round the gaol-house, murmuring menace like bees at a barbeque – or possums in a bakery, as Phineas might have put it.

There could, you'd have thought, be no mistaking

their intentions; although, in fact, Eddie Foy, who was just leaving the stagedoor, did have the brief impression that they wanted his autograph. On second thoughts, however, he decided he'd best let his agent handle that kind of thing in future; and he went rapidly back inside, to smarten up the tricky bit in the second act. But I digress . . .

The Doctor presently noticed that the crowd carried Steven, trussed like a rupture, amongst them; and it soon became obvious that he was no willing participant in the proceedings.

'You still in there, Holliday?' called Ike, who had become the spokesman by general agreement.

Wyatt sighed. He'd been through all this sort of thing before, and knew most of the lines by heart . . .

'Get off the street, Clanton,' he advised. 'The Doc's my prisoner!'

Ike knew all about that, of course, and wasn't disposed to waste time arguing the rights and wrongs of the case.

'That's too bad, Marshal,' he sympathised, 'because, if he ain't out here quicker 'n you can . . . you can . . .'

'Skin a ring-tailed 'coon?' Phineas suggested.

'That's right . . . skin a ring-tailed 'coon,' Ike agreed, 'then his friend Regret's gonna swing in his place! An' bein' the fine old Southern gentleman he is, I'll bet Doc wouldn't want that.'

He was dead right, of course . . . But, on the other hand . . . Well, I mean . . .

'What can I do?' asked the Doctor. 'Shall I go out and explain to them?'

'Wouldn't advise it,' commented Earp. 'Them boys ain't accustomed to the cut an' thrust of rhetorical logic. Their talk,' he amplified, 'is as the crackling of thorns under a pot...'

'But if I don't go, they'll hang Steven; you heard him say so...'

'An' if you do go, they'll hang you along of him. 'Sides of which, I need 'em to continue believin' as you're Holliday for a while, so don't go tellin' 'em different! Not that they'd believe you anywise, but don't try it! No... I'll think of something... pretty well bound to...'

'Time's runnin' out, Marshal,' called Ike, having worked out how long three men could reasonably occupy themselves in skinning a 'coon. 'What's it gonna be?'

Being personally concerned, Steven now decided he would like to say something.

'Stay where you are, Doctor,' he advised, 'they're bluffing!'

'You think that, boy, you're gonna be powerful surprised, any moment now,' growled Phineas; and, at the third attempt, he succeeded in throwing the unoccupied end of the rope over a convenient branch of the hanging-tree – not as simple an operation as you might think... at least, not with Phineas on noose.

'Well, what about it?' persevered Ike. 'You all a-comin', or ain't you?'

He was beginning to fear an anti-climax, and after all, he had his standing with the mob to consider...

But Wyatt had now thought, and was well-pleased with the result. An unoriginal scheme, perhaps, but it had always gone down well before...

'You keep 'em talking, Bat – and I'll try to work round behind 'em.'

'Ain't that jest a mite corny?' asked the Sheriff. 'I mean, law-men's forever doin' such...'

100

'Well, because it works, that's why! Now, don't get me all riled up, when I'm trying to concentrate!'

And he slipped out of the building by the rear entrance – or exit, rather.

Now, you must picture the scene; because, if you don't, all this will mean nothing. On one side of the street is the gaol-house, right? And directly opposite is the hanging-tree, famed in legend. But *between* them – and this is important – is the milling mob, carrying those blazing torches; unnecessarily, you'd have thought, since it was a fine moonlit night – but, for whatever reason, they had 'em. And this, as you will readily appreciate, had the fortunate effect of throwing the tree into shadow.

Yes, it did – if you work it out. Well, comparative shadow, anyway ... (Look, who's telling this tale, you or me? Don't give me no argument, right?) And of this *shadow*, I say, Wyatt took advantage ...

We have previously remarked the circuitous manner in which the late Seth Harper moseyed down Main Street; and now the Marshal adopted a somewhat similar technique – although, being a law-man, the effect was, of course, far more dignified. Happily, no one, in fact, *did* notice this effect – because that would have negated the whole time-honoured manoeuvre – and pretty soon he was in a position to make, as the saying is, his play. And not a moment *too* soon, either – because the one weak point in the strategy was that Bat was supposed to keep them talking; and he wasn't particularly good at that sort of thing ...

'Heard a good one the other day,' he volunteered, at length. 'Seems there was this feller, Bob Ford, got himself behind Jesse James ...'

Wyatt groaned. Trust Bat to give the whole plan

101

away . . .

And the crowd groaned likewise, because they'd heard it . . .

However, it's an ill wind, et cetera . . . because, in so doing, they conveniently covered the sound of Wyatt's galloping the final straight, to the tree; swiping the unsuspecting Phineas sideways with his Buntline Special – pistol-whipping, it's called, a favourite technique of his, by all accounts – and finally cutting through Steven's rope . . . Game, set, and match!

'Now then, Sinners,' he purred, 'shall we continue the discussion from here? No? Then how about: the next man as moves, gets it? You gonna be first, Billy?'

But fire-eating Billy had his excuse-me right to hand . . .

'If you wasn't wearing a badge, Marshal!' he explained, and left the threat tactfully unspoken.

'That's *why* I wear it,' said Wyatt, modestly.

'And if you wasn't caught in a cross-fire, Billy,' called Bat as he breathed heavily along the double barrels of a shot-gun. 'Lynchin' party's over, folks!'

Well, that's about all there was to it, really. The crowd agreed that there seemed to be nothing much to wait around for; and began to drift back where it came from, wondering why in hell things always turned out like this. Although, to do him justice, Ike seemed disposed to stick it out for a while longer.

Wyatt discouraged him.

'All's left to do is talk big an' look foolish, Clanton – get goin'!'

'Not without Phin, I don't,' said the chap-fallen bad-man.

'Your brother ain't available, right now,' explained Wyatt, 'on account, he's under arrest. Attempted

hangin',' he elaborated further. 'Less'n you're fixin' to
join him, I'd go home to your Pa. You too, Billy.'

The brothers looked at each other. Yes, that was a
thought – Pa! The prospective mayor wasn't going to
like this!

To add to their pleasure, Charlie the bar-keep now
approached, bearing tidings...

'Mr Clanton, sir – an' you too Mr Clanton: I gotta tell
you – that ain't Doc Holliday that's bein' held in there!'

Well, this may not have been the anti-climax Ike had
been fearing – he'd already had that one – but this was
another. And it was a beauty!

He narrowed his eyes, accordingly.

And so did the Marshal...

17

Pa Clanton Keeps A Welcome

It was Wyatt's inclination to tell Charlie to mind his own damn' business; but what with keeping a grip on the buffaloed Phineas, holding a gun where it would do most good; and, simultaneously, trying to explain to Steven how you untie a running bow-line, – for pity's sake! – he was ... Well, you can't be everywhere, can you?

'What gives you that idea, Charlie?' Ike asked. 'You been at the sauce bottle?'

Well he had ... but even so ...

'Because it's like the old guy kept tryin' to tell you,' he announced. 'He ain't by no means the same Doctor ... as ... as this other Doctor, whom he ain't! Seems like he's another mess o' hog-swill entirely!'

'You funnin', Charlie?' asked Billy. 'Because if so, I'm fresh out o' laughs!'

''Tain't no laughin' matter,' denied Charlie, 'on account this altogether different Doctor, Holliday by name, the *real* one, he's jest been in my bar ... an' if I'm drunk, as you so kindly imply, then your friend Seth Harper's still alive ... which ain't so! Holliday shot him clean as a dude's trousers. Fastest thing I ever saw –

which is pretty fast, considerin' what goes on in my place, since you boys hit town! So, I jest thought I'd best stop you gettin' up against the law, all over nothin' . . .'

'Thanks!' said Ike, grimly. 'We're surely obliged . . .'

And Charlie blew – secure in the satisfaction of a job well done . . .

'So,' said Billy, 'you knew all along the old guy weren't Holliday, did you, Earp? That's clear contrary to the natural, clear course of dad-blasted justice, ain't it now?'

'Try sayin' Marshal, and rememberin' it, too! I don't have to answer to you, Billy. I'll justify my actions to the Citizens' Committee, if I have to. Now, walk away, while you still got the equipment!'

'I ain't takin' no orders from no sanctimonious . . .'

'Leave it, Billy,' counselled his brother. 'Cussin' ain't called for. Marshal's jest about all through givin' orders! By the time Pa gits through with him, he'll lose his badge so fast, it'll . . . it'll . . .'

But Phineas was in no condition to help him find *le mot juste*. So, mumbling mechanically, the boys backed up and off, towards where the sunset would have been if it hadn't been over.

Where the sunset used to be was now the Clanton Ranch; and the difference was immediately apparent. For one thing, whereas the sunset had been a golden testament of glory, and poets had said so, the ranch fell somewhat short of this high standard in several respects, and everybody said so. 'Squalid' was the word they generally used. Pa Clanton claimed he kept it that way in memory of his wife, God rest her tongue, whose early death had followed hard upon her premature burial, back in '75.

You could still see her temporary grave near the blocked over-flow from the hog-pound, if you weren't careful; and along about now of an evening, it was the old man's habit to wander gladly down there, and get in some spitting practice – a thing he hadn't hardly got enough of when she was alive.

It was at these times of solitude he would remember his early pioneering days, when he had trecked West to carve out a false name for himself, far from her father's shot-gun; and also with what soulless devotion she and the Pinkertons' men had finally tracked him down to this blessed corner of nowhere.

But now he was alone in the world; apart, that is to say, from his four fine boys – no, three now, he chuckled to remember – who seemed to be doing their damndedest to remind him of her. Still, they were all he'd got, Heaven help him; so, tossing a bunch of poison-ivy onto the hallowed mound, he strode – briskly, for a man with his unpleasant diseases – back to the chill intimacy of his old colonial kitchen – so called, because the termites were into it in a big way – to see if they were home yet.

Rightly speaking, he considered, there should have been big doin's in town this day; and, by now, Holliday should be gracing a trestle-table in the cold-store at Jackson's Hardware – so often pressed into service as ante-room to the infernal hot-spot.

And with the demon dentist thus occupied, why, the way would be clear for an undisturbed final confrontation with the more properly constituted authorities; for Earp and Masterson, he judged, were now all that stood between him and the mayoral parlour, with

106

its bright vistas of graft and civic corruption, plus a complimentary pass to Ma Golightly's.

So he was a mite discountenanced to find no-one in residence bar his yellow hound dog, which was gnawing a disused buffalo skull on the groaning table. Absent-mindedly, he removed man's best friend with a bull-whip; whereupon it bit him affectionately on one of his numbed ankles, en route for the Great Outdoors. They understood each other, these two – having many points in common.

He was therefore engaged in plastering varmint-fat on the probably rabid cicatrice, when he heard the sound for which his ears were already half-cocked – that of horses' hooves in something of a hurry; and he limped over to the mullioned arrow-slit, his over-crowded countenance a-gleam with dubious welcome.

Three horses cantered into the dung-encrusted yard – a feature of the property commonly referred to as the unpleasance – but only, he was puzzled to note, two riders. The medium-sized, bearded boy was missing.

'Where's Phin?' he enquired, after a recount. 'Stayed on in town fer a few laughs, an' such?'

Damn! Ike had been hoping the subject would not be touched on till after a few words of conventional greeting. 'Well, I'll tell you . . .' he said, dismounting abruptly, and picking himself up. 'Or maybe Billy here would rather . . .?'

Billy waived the privilege. 'You're the eldest,' he said, 'best get it over . . .'

They edged into the house past Pa's doom-exuding bulk, and settled themselves side by side on the parlour hitching-rail. They put Pa in mind of two turkey-buzzards at a christening . . .

'Go on,' he said, grimly, 'where's he at this time?'

107

'Properly speaking,' said Ike, 'I cain't rightly say; but its a fair bet that by now he's in the gaol-house.'

'Reckon he'd have sent word hisself,' contributed Billy, ''cept that he was handicapped by havin' been a mite pole-axed . . .'

'That's it,' agreed Ike, 'same like a herd-bull in a stockyard.'

'Oh?' said Pa, putting himself under restraint, and counting to five with some difficulty. 'And by whom if I may put the question?'

'Earp,' said Ike.

'Put your goddamned hand in front of your mouth when you do that!' said his parent. And then light dawned, with the beginning of a bright side . . . 'You mean, Wyatt took him in fer killin' Holliday? That's it now, ain't it?'

'Well now, Pa – I cain't tell you that, because it ain't rightly so.'

He had read all about George Washington, and his little hat-check cutie; and he admired the man in consequence . . .

'You see, time Phin got hisself incommoded, we was seemingly after the wrong guy . . .'

'Go on,' said Pa. 'You tell it, Billy.'

'There you go, Pa,' said Billy, 'An' time we-all was a-doin' that, the *right* guy – the *real* Holliday, that is – was engaged in shootin' the dyin' night-shades out of Seth Harper!'

'That's about all really, Pa,' Ike resumed; ''cept that I'd like to say, it could have happened to anyone. You got to give us that . . .'

Pa knew what he'd like to give them, but couldn't rightly see any point in it at this juncture. 'Sides of which he was fresh out of wasp poison. No, comes a time when a father has to realise he's accidentally sired a brood-pen full of pea-brained gophers; and all he can do then is make the best of it.

Nevertheless, he thought a word or two of some sort might be in season.

'Seth Harper,' he complained, 'owes me money!'

'Don't rightly see how you aim to collect it...' said Billy.

'Seems like I done paid him all of one hundred confederate dollars to back you up, an' get Holliday. An' now that's cash down the cess-pit, ain't it?'

'There you go!' admitted Billy again.

'Don't keep sayin' that! God knows where you pick up these expressions! So I tell you what you do now, 'cause it seems a Pa has to look out fer his young-uns, regardless of lack of affection! I'm a-gonna give you five hundred more; an' you will take that small fortune to procure me the services of a *real* gun-man. Go get me Johnny Ringo!' he hissed.

The boys reeled with apprehension. 'Johnny Ringo! Now, just hold on there...'

'Ringo rides alone, Pa – you know that!' said Billy. 'On account of no-one durst ride with him! So what makes you think as he'd throw in with us?'

'Five hundred dollars says so,' said Pa, confidently. 'An' seein' it's Ringo, I'd best made 'em Yankee dollars. Now – go git him!'

'Don't rightly know where he's at,' objected Ike. 'You know what that class of man is like? They ride the wild wind in search of new, blue yonders; where there's no fence-posts, or whatever.'

'Then ask around, boy – such time as I've still left you a tongue in your head! Seein' as my union with your late Ma has been blessed with a litter of no-account, droop-

109

eared lap-dogs, seems I require the services of a top-gun! So go git me Ringo,' he persevered; and his voice rose to an apoplectic scream, just in time to add, 'An' git him here fast!'

So, realising he was serious, the boys made a boot-assisted exit, put their horses into rapid reverse, and went to ask around.

18

Ringo in the Morning

Crimson-fingered dawn was lighting the hoose-gow as with a blow-torch – for it was a fine morning – when the Doctor and Steven, aged by a night of twitching sleep in which dreams of tight neck-wear featured prominently, emerged from their respective cells to find Wyatt and Bat examining Phineas Clanton's creased, Neanderthal skull with some distaste.

'Is he conscious yet?' asked the Doctor.

'Difficult to tell,' diagnosed Bat. 'Looks like he may be alive; but, if so, he ain't gonna enjoy it for a while . . .'

'Really, Marshal,' protested the Doctor, 'was it necessary to hit the man quite so hard?'

'Yes, after all he was only going to hang me,' said Steven. 'Doctor, it wasn't *your* neck in the noose last night. I, for one, am very grateful to Mr Earp!'

'I was only the instrument of Divine Justice, I reckon,' demurred Wyatt, modestly. Over the years, he had grown used to accusations of police provocation, and had learnt to pay them no never mind. 'Maybe you don't realise how close that was out there? For what we did not receive, may the Lord make us truly thankful.'

'Well, of course we are,' agreed the Doctor, 'but

surely there are other ways of doing these things?'

Wyatt considered the question. ''Spose I could've shot him – but seein' I got no definite instructions to that effect from On High, I saw fit to let the transgressor have the benefit of Jehovah's everlastin' mercy ...'

They looked at this evidence of Big J's clemency, and decided to let the matter drop. After all, the Lord had done it now, and there it was ...

'Well,' said the Doctor, 'I fear that my friend and I will not be present to witness the outcome of this unfortunate affair. As soon as we have collected Dodo from the hotel, we must be on our way.'

'Well, Hallelujah!' said Wyatt. 'Maybe once you're gone, the town'll settle down some.'

And so, with mutual expressions of good-will and relief, they parted – but only for the time being ...

Because little did they know that an hour previous to this valedictory chat, a stranger had clinked and jingled his menacing way into the Last Chance Saloon where he had taken up the position at the bar so recently occupied by the late Seth Harper.

And you could say he filled it better, at that; on account of this weren't no ordinary two-bit, snake-eyed, back-shooting delinquent – no, sir! Not by a vulture's gut, it weren't!

By one of those coincidences without which even the best fiction would be unreadable, and even a true story such as this, unconvincing, what we have here is the cool and deadly, calm and imperturbable, et cetera, high-class, professional gun-slinger, Johnny Ringo; before whom strong men would have quailed, if he'd ever given them a moment to get on with it.

A killer of the old school, in fact.

Yes, but hold on there – there weren't no malice about it – or not a lot, anyway. A business occupation, it was; and not just an unpleasant hobby. The way he looked at it, he was kind of working his way through college: because the one thing he'd always envied Doc Holliday – whom, in all other respects, he disliked – was his education. But, whereas Doc, as we know, was a medical man, Ringo himself had preferred to opt for the Classics, on account he considered them to be a mite more genteel. And to this end, it was his invariable habit to devote some percentage of his blood money to the purchase of such texts in the dead languages as were considered to be required reading by the folks who live on Nob Hill.

At the moment he was into Caesar's *Gallic Wars*, and he considered this well-reviewed, ten-volume, high-tone work to be a lulu, in every respect: action, human interest, and class, in that order. O.K. – so it strained his saddle-bags some; but long as it lent his conversation that sparkle and polish so widely esteemed by the cognoscenti – what the hell? Because one day he might meet some of the latter; and then just watch his smoke! So, you will gather, that besides being one of the most efficient life-extinguishers a prospective mayor could wish to employ, he was a sure enough odd-ball. And, bearing in mind the traditional hostility between Science and the Arts, should he and Holliday ever meet face to face on their opposing paths to perdition, then any innocent by-standers in the vicinity had better watch out for themselves, that's all!

Now, since he was dressed from head to foot in black; and since dawn, as we have already recorded, was still an hour off; and since Charlie had the shakes, and attributed the jingle of spurs to the tinkling of the ice in his breakfast – for all these reasons, the bar-keep did not at once notice Ringo, looming in the nervous shadows as he was, like a promise of the wrath to come.

But at length the irritated tapping of a gun-butt in a bowl of the nuts you love to crunch awakened him to the fact that custom was in the offing; and he slouched gracelessly forward to inform the intruder that the bar wasn't open yet.

'So open it,' suggested Ringo, pleasantly; and he leaned across the bar to light a cheroot from a match struck on Charlie's unshaven jowl.

'Now see here . . .' Charlie was beginning, when the flaring lucifer illuminated the pale and intellectual, pock-marked physiognomy before him. And, with no pleasure at all, he recognised it.

'And fetch me a double, straight,' continued Ringo, completing his esteemed order.

'Yes, sir, Mr Ringo – right away! Double, straight, coming right up, sir . . . ;' and he busied himself about the matter, to the accompaniment of a certain amount of tooth-chattering.

'How come you know my name?' asked Johnny, cautiously.

'Why, Mr Ringo, I guess near about everybody . . . I mean, well, I sure enough *heard* about you, sir . . .'

'What have you heard?'

Careful now, Charlie, careful . . . Don't tell him *that*, for God's sake!

'Well now, sir, seems to me it was only last night a couple of boys was askin' after you . . . 'long around midnight, it was . . .'

'That so? And who was they?'

'Far as I remember, sir, it was Ike and Billy Clanton.

114

Maybe you know 'em?'

'Can't say I do. *What* was they askin'?'

'Well,' – he lowered his voice – 'they was sayin' as their Pa would give you five hundred if you'd throw in with 'em against Wyatt Earp...'

'Against the Marshal? Then you can tell 'em I take *seven* hundred for a law-man.'

He calculated that with the extra two, he could maybe get himself the complete Orations of Demosthenes, in genuine Morocco...

'Surely will, Mr Ringo – it'll be a pleasure! An' shall I also tell 'em as you'll be ridin' out there? I mean, I can easy draw you a little map, showin' you where the ranch is...'

'In my own good time I'll maybe go. Say I got business of my own to settle first. Personal business, with Doc Holliday.'

'You have? Well now, excuse me, Mr Ringo – an' of course I know it ain't nothin' to do with me – but I reckon that'll suit 'em jest fine; 'cause they're layin' for Holliday too!'

Ringo spat like a cobra. 'Then here's another thing you can tell 'em, boy: tell 'em, Holliday's mine! I ain't trailed him all the way from Fort Griffin, to have some bunch of uneducated hoodlums foul it up! Understand me?'

'I certainly do, Mr Ringo – an' I'm sure they'll be happy to accommodate you there! Why, they missed him only yesterday, in this very bar!'

'Holliday was here?'

'In a pig's ear, he was!'

'What?'

'Just an expression. Why, he shot down the late Seth Harper, right where you're standin' now! Then he lit out o' town with his two fancy women, same as though all the devils in hell was after him!'

'One of 'em is! So who's his company?'

'There was two of 'em, like I say. Pert little party, name of Dodo Dupont – who's a singer. And an older girl, called Kate, who's somethin' in the same line; when she ain't otherwise occupied, if you follow me, Mr Ringo.'

'I hear you real fine. Mind tellin' me if this here Kate also goes under the name of Elder?'

'Sure does – or leastways, always *has*. Now I hear, she's about to change it. She's fixin' to marry Holliday, she tells me.'

Uncharacteristically, Ringo slopped his drink.

'That truly so? Fetch me another of those, an' fast! In fact, you'll oblige me by leavin' the bottle.'

'Why, certainly, Mr Ringo – and it's on the house!'

'Never supposed no different. What's your name, boy?'

'Charlie, sir . . .'

'Then, here's lookin' at you, Charlie . . .'

Charlie wished he wouldn't.

Ringo drank off a half-tumbler; and for some reason, felt better. Kate could rot in hell, for all he cared. In fact, he'd prefer it.

'Thank you, sir. Why, I jest cain't wait to see the Marshal's face, when he hears *you're* goin' against him, Mr Ringo!'

Ringo forgot about Kate and her prospects for the moment.

'You plannin' to tell him, maybe?'

'Well, of course not, Mr Ringo! I was only sayin' . . .'

'Charlie, Charlie,' sighed Ringo, sadly, 'I know your kind. You say too much . . .'

'No, sir; I won't say nothin' to nobody!'

'Now, ain't that the truth, Charlie?' Ringo agreed – and shot him through the throat. Just like that.

And he carried his drink over to a pleasant table near the window to reread that exciting bit in Volume Two, where Caesar carves up Gaul into three parts. And he was thus engaged, when Steven and the Doctor came in.

19

Post Mortem

They were in high, or at least somewhat elevated, spirits. Escaping from a lynch mob will sometimes do that for you.

And now the TARDIS, with all its promise of more sophisticated disasters to come, beckoned them backwards. All that was left for them to do was to collect Dodo, tell her how brave they'd been and then fly off to health and happiness in some galactic cataclysm. Fine, and also dandy – if you care for that sort of thing!

'Intrepid' is the word which suits them, at this point. Why, they were even whistling 'The Happy Wanderer', which just shows you...

So they approached Charlie – who, for some reason, was slumped across the reception-desk – and clearing their throats, and pleased to be able to do so, they asked for their keys.

He was quite obviously not thinking on his feet this morning, and ignored the simple request.

'Dear me,' said the Doctor, 'the man is incapable of performing his duties!' Which is one way of putting it, I suppose...

'Asleep at his post,' said Steven. 'Dangerous, I'd have

thought, in a place like this.' And he shook Charlie by the shoulder.

Apart from disturbing a couple of blue-tail flies who had thought the site ripe for development, this did nothing but reveal a spreading pool of blood on the hotel register; which proceeded to find its own level, and drip into the ullage.

'Great Heavens, he seems to be dead!' diagnosed the Doctor.

The corpse's lolling head appeared to nod in confirmation, as Charlie continued his interrupted journey to the grass roots.

'Heart failure...' suggested Ringo, from his break-fast nook. 'High livin' an' hard liquor don't pay...'

'Don't be ridiculous!' said Steven. 'He's been shot! Look – you can see where the bullet... where the bullet... Excuse me a moment...' And he utilised the sink for his own purposes...

'But this is outrageous!' complained the Doctor. 'He had no business whatever to get himself killed! He should have been guarding Dodo with his life, a man in his position!'

A man in Charlie's position wasn't rightly able to guard anything much, save maybe a few earthworms. But nevertheless, Ringo took the cue.

'Looks like he already done that,' he said: and thought he might as well hoist a little Latin up the gallows, to see if anyone would swing from it.

'*Quis custodiet ipsos custodes?*' he drawled. There was a surprised pause. Ah, well... 'Which means,' he sighed, 'who's gonna look after the goddam guards?' (A favourite gag of Caesar's, by all accounts.)

'There is absolutely no need to translate,' said the Doctor, 'I know perfectly well what you mean. After all,

119

Sapientia urbs conditur, as you may have heard.'

'What?' asked Steven, returning when empty.

'A city is founded on wisdom, my boy! How pleasant to meet an educated man at last!'

'Likewise, I'm sure,' said Johnny, lighting up like the fourth of July in Chicago. This was it! The intellectual soulmate he'd been waiting for! Suddenly all those long hours bent over a hot vocabulary had been worth it!

'So *requiescat in pace*, hey?' he crowed, flipping a coin onto Charlie's stomach. 'Towards the funeral,' he explained, *'De mortuis nil nisi bonum!'*

'What?' said Steven, again.

'Nothin's too good for a goddam corpse,' said Ringo. 'That's about it, ain't it, friend?' he asked the Doctor.

'Well, in a somewhat loose version of the idiomatic vernacular, I suppose...' the Doctor agreed. 'But surely, my dear fellow, rather than voicing such flowery exequies, we should be asking ourselves who can possibly have committed this completely unjustified homicide?'

'Not much question about that, I'd say,' volunteered the conscienceless Ringo, blandly. 'Seems like that Doc Holliday won't never mend his uncivilised, medical-school ways!'

'Holliday?' snapped the Doctor, not wishing much to be reminded of the man. 'What's he got to do with it?'

'Only man in the territory low enough to shoot an unarmed bar-keep, I'd say. Open and shut case,' Ringo continued. 'Moreover, I heard he was in here last night, lookin' fer trouble, like always; which jest about clinches it, don't it?'

'Then where is he now? He must be apprehended at once!'

'Seems like he's done taken off on his law-dodgin'

travels once more. Anxious to avoid his just retribution,' he clarified. 'Come to think of it, I heard tell he was keepin' company with a couple of high-steppin' saloon gals. Ain't it the truth, how such women'll drag a man to damnation?'

'*Two*, do you say?' enquired the Doctor, quivering with moral outrage.

'Two,' confirmed Ringo. 'The man is a monster of lewdness and debauchery, an insatiable satyr, who will brook no restraint on his vile appetites!'

Some prod-nose, Cicero probably, had once applied these terms of opprobrium to Julius Caesar, he recollected; and he had always fancied they would come in useful one day.

But Steven's mind had pounced on what it suspected was more than a coincidence.

'Two?' he enquired, in his turn. 'You don't happen to know their names, do you?'

'Well now,' pondered Ringo – or appeared to ponder. 'Give me a moment, an' maybe I'll come up with something ... Why, sure – seems like one of 'em goes under the name of Kate Elder ...'

'Holliday's receptionist!' the Doctor remembered.

'Receptionist? Well, I've heard as she does kinda keep open house ...'

'But the other one?' urged Steven. 'What was *her* name?'

'Hold on, there – let me see ... Somethin' with a flavour of frenchified dressin' to it ... Why, a Miss Dodo Dupont, I do believe!'

The time travellers reeled in consternation! This was all they needed: Dodo on the lam, with a wanted killer, and a bar-room floozie! The morning, which had tiptoed in with all the happy panache of a State Funeral, was bidding fair to remain roughly on course...

'Oh God!' exclaimed Steven. 'There's nothing for it – we'll just have to go and find them!'

'You don't say? Forgive me askin', but this here Gallic flibbertigibbet's a close friend o' yours, maybe?'

'Yes, dammit!' admitted Steven. 'Confound her innocent, artless little ways!'

Ringo felt much the same about Kate and thought he understood. So he expressed friendly and sympathetic interest.

'So, if you find 'em, friends, what are you fixin' to do? Figure on gunnin' Holliday down, is that it?'

'Certainly not!' said the Doctor. 'He is my dentist. But it is essential that we get Dodo back; and so we shall ... we shall just have to reason with him to that effect ...'

'Now that I'd truly like to see! Because, seein' as we talk the same dead language, I'll tell you folks somethin' ... Seems like you an' me's got common cause against Holliday ... Same like we're bound to have against all forces of ignorance an' oppression, the world over! So now, jest supposin', young feller, I was to let you ride with me?'

'You mean, you know where they are?' interrupted Steven.

'Reckon I can maybe calculate same. The Doc generally leaves a trail like a herd of waltzing caribou when he's pushed!'

'Then we should be extremely grateful for your assistance,' said the Doctor.

Ringo smiled like a scar. 'Proud to be of service! There's jest one thing: kindred spirits as we may be, you get yourself between me an' him, boy, an' I'll blast you down, soon as spit at you! Remember that?'

Steven promised he'd bear it in mind. And it was further arranged that the Doctor would be more gainfully employed by staying where he damn' well was for once; because it might not be a bad idea, at that, if he was to tell Wyatt Earp of the march of events.

And so this is how it came about, that shortly thereafter, a passing vulture observed Two-gun Steven Regret, Terror of the Spaceways, in company with his new partner, Johnny Ringo, Death's understudy and master of the Latin tag, swallowing Holliday's dust on the trail to Purgatory Bend.

The vulture followed along. After all, you never knew . . .

20

Thought for Feud

After their departure, the Doctor trudged glumly back to the nerve-centre of crime prevention and law enforcement; and was surprised to find himself in the presence of, not one, but a whole confabulation of Earps! Which wasn't no glee party, neither . . . because herein lies a sadness . . .

Wyatt's call for reinforcements had been answered right speedily by the rest of the clan; who had at once dropped whatever criminal they'd happened to be beating the nonsense out of at the time, and ridden in from all available points of the compass. Nothing remarkable in that: it's what brothers do when one of their number becomes a mite over-extended. As witness the Clantons, on the extension to his full length of the departed Reuben.

So now Virgil Earp, the eldest, was here; and Warren Earp was here; and Morgan Earp, the youngest, was also among those present: with the trifling difference, in the case of the latter, that he was now dead as a beetled elm tree; which, strictly speaking, made him no age at all.

Added to which, Virgil had got himself a dose of buck-shot in his gun-arm; a thing which will generally slow you down some. So, at a rough estimate, that left Warren as the only functional addition to the strength of the angels.

Near as one can tell, in face of the conflicting reports lately current, what had happened was this – or near enough.

The previous night, Ike and Billy Clanton, having left their message for Ringo, were riding home full of zip and buck, to announce to their proud parent that when it came to a matter of asking around, they were the best available. And, in this exalted frame of mind, they had encountered young Morgan who, rightly speaking, shouldn't have been out that late, as he was riding in from Dodge.

Words had been exchanged; and, since these were in no way civil, bullets had swiftly followed. Which, at those odds, and considering Morgan's inexperience, had made the outcome as inevitable as the Clantons had calculated. A fine, old fashioned bush-wacking, in fact.

It was while they were examining their trophy, that Virgil had ridden up, to enquire – remember, it was dark, and the parties had not previously met – if he could be of any assistance.

'Sure!' they said, 'Hold this!' And they had blasted him from the saddle with a shot-gun they happened to have along. Leaving him for dead, they had then tittupped onwards; confident that their subsequent debriefing by Pa would be an occasion for joy, not unmired with gladness. And, after a pause for stock-taking, Virgil had pulled as much of himself together as he could find, and ridden in with both the news and his brother's body.

It was just this time that the Doctor chose to come a-calling.

Always a forbidding figure, Wyatt now put the Doctor in mind of a chariot of wrath, forming deep thunderclouds on its way to preside at The Last Judgement, with something of a hangover!

'That does it!' Wyatt hissed. 'Bat – drag Phineas in here – and I don't mean gentle!'

Phineas, now restored to what, in his case, passed for consciousness, had been an interested audience to Virgil's story and was consequently apprehensive.

'It warn't my fault!' he claimed; 'You know I bin here all night – sleepin' like a ... like a ...' What in hell was innocent when it slept? 'Like a snow-bound gopher!' he finally achieved. 'You cain't take it out on me!'

'He's right, Wyatt,' warned Bat. 'He's a prisoner in legal custody! We don't want no crusadin' gaol-reform articles, on top of all!'

'I ain't gonna hurt him none,' said Wyatt, grimly. 'Know what I'm gonna do with you?' he asked the palsied captive.

'What?' enquired Phineas, interested in spite of himself.

'Why, I'm gonna open the door, an' let you walk right out of here. How about that?'

'You can't do that, either,' Bat objected. 'I tell you, he's a ...'

'Aimin' to stop me, Bat?'

'Well, no, Wyatt – but I thought I'd best mention it ...'

'You crazy?' asked Warren. 'There's more than enough Clantons out there, the way it is!'

'Don't tell me nothin' about the Clantons, Warren! Don't even breathe their foul name!' He turned back to Phineas. 'An' *when* you get outside, boy; soon as the bright air of freedom is a-bubblin' in your nostrils, I want fer you to ride on out to your Pa, an' give him a message from me!'

'What'll I say?' enquired Phineas, anxious to get it right.

'Tell him that come sun-up tomorrow, me an' Warren an' Bat'll be waitin' fer him an' the rest of his hell-spawn at the O.K. Corral! Say it loud an' clear, Phineas, with none of your lame-brain fer-instances. An' as fer you, boy, I surely do eagerly anticipate seein' you over my gun-barrel on that occasion. Now, *git*!' And he booted the bearded master of epigram clear through the door, into the middle of the morning.

'Ahem!' said the Doctor, feeling it was time he joined the discussion.

'Yes, the old guy's right,' said Bat. 'Guess you jest summed it up, partner! Wyatt, this ain't by no means according to Hoyle! What you're doin' is declarin' a private war! You cain't do that, not if you're a law-man!'

'Then here's my badge,' said Wyatt, grandly, removing his badge and unfortunately a piece of his shirt in the process. If it wasn't one thing, it was another. 'Time's all out for the niceties of lawful miscarriage of justice, wouldn't you say?'

'Then this time, I cain't go along with you,' said Bat, sadly. 'I won't go agin' you, Wyatt, on account of our long an' friendly association; but I cain't no-wise back you up!'

The ex-Marshal breathed deeply; a patient man, incommoded by a knife in the back. 'Then it's me an' Warren,' he concluded. 'Reckon we can take care of it.'

'You still got me,' groaned Virgil. 'Guess I can still tote a shot-gun. Fact is, it'd pleasure me some ...'

'Ride on home, Virgil,' instructed Wyatt. 'Don't want no cripples lousin' things up,' he explained, kindly. 'No – the man I need here right now is Doc Holliday!'

'Who, I believe, you jest ran out o' town,' pointed out Bat. 'An' a good thing, too! Start consortin' with that kind, in a doin's like this, an' you'd be branded with the same iron! That's *all* you need, right now!'

'If I may say something,' interjected the Doctor, glad to be able to make a contribution at last, 'I think you may find he will shortly be on his way. My friend, Steven, set off to find him this morning.'

'Small chance of his doin' that, I'd say, when he don't know the territory.'

'Ah, but he had a local connection with him who was kind enough to offer assistance. I think we may have every confidence in the gentleman.'

'Yeah? An' so who might that be?' enquired Wyatt, at a loss to account for a gentleman being in the neighbourhood at this time, or indeed ever.

'Unfortunately I forgot to enquire his name. But he was extremely helpful, and appeared to be well-educated. In fact, he conducted part of our conversation in Latin!'

At this annoucement, a series of hair-line cracks appeared in Wyatt's baroque façade, such as would have given an architectural conservationist, had one been present, food for alarmed thought.

'Johnny Ringo!' he breathed.

'Ah, so you know the man? Is he a friend of yours?'

'Ringo's a friend of nobody,' Bat explained, 'except, maybe, the devil! He's a bounty-hunting shootist – sells himself to the highest bidder.'

'And as of now,' confirmed Wyatt, 'that'll likely be the Clantons! Moreover, him an' Doc's got old scores to settle, concernin' the possession of Kate Elder's provocative person! And you sent him out there to find them?'

'Well, it seemed to be a good idea at the time...' faltered the Doctor, 'in view of the shooting of the hotel manager...' he amplified.

But this was altogether too much for Wyatt, who had a pretty full dossier, at the moment.

'Then, little friend of all the world,' he said pleasantly, 'here's another good idea for you to chaw on. If it turns out as Doc *cain't* take care of Ringo, come sun-up tomorrow I'm gonna be shy a gun-hand; an' I'm gonna need me a replacement. An' since half the town is already of the opinion that you an' Holliday is one an' the same ... if I was you, I'd get in a little practice on the equaliser!'

21

Dodo Draws a Bead

Coincident with the above conversation, an unprecedented event was occurring someplace else;
namely the back room of Clancy's renowned Elysian
Fields Flop-House and Grill (Bath one dollar extra);
and in this Ritz-Carlton of Purgatory Bend, Doc
Holliday was being beaten to the draw.

Mind you, he had every excuse, his hands being
currently encumbered by a tray-full of Clancy's bas-
cuisine – crawdad chowder and mash, if you want to
know – but still . . . Try as he would, he could not off-
hand recall a similar happenstance; and you could say it
rankled.

Moreover, the fire-arm now waving at will in the
general direction of his midriff was held in the
inexperienced grip of one whom he had hitherto
counted amongst his dwindling circle of friends. That
would teach him to trust people, he thought.

'Hands up!' said Dodo.

'Well now,' he temporised, 'if I do that, then these
high-priced victuals is a-goin' to slop all over the
flowered linoleum.'

'All right then, *half*-way up,' she agreed, making a

concession.

'Have you any particular motive in makin' so free with these fool-hardy instructions?' he asked her. 'Or is you jest passin' the time of day?'

'You promised you'd take me back to my friends this morning,' she explained, 'and here it is, lunchtime. I am no longer prepared to tolerate this kind of shilly-shallying; and I now insist that we hit the trail. Are you ready to start?'

As we know, Doc had privately decided, in view of everything, to give Tombstone and its hostile purlieus the miss for the foreseeable. So he prevaricated.

'Little lady, I'm ready to leap like a mountain goat, you ever do somethin' like this again! May I enquire further what you are a-fixin' to do with that there instrument of bloody destruction; which is, rightly speaking, the trousseau of my intended?'

'Shoot you, if you force me to adopt such a course!'

Doc had suspected as much.

'Then will you kindly declare, here and now, whether you have ever in your sweet life handled that class of weapon before?'

'No – but I *am* familiar with the principle of its operation. You pull the trigger, I believe?'

'That's about it, I reckon. So then, how would you propose to rejoin your loved ones?'

'I shall try not to kill you. I am aiming for your right arm. I have already drawn a bead on it.'

'You have? Then I would like to point out that right now you got me in the thoracic cavity. Where my heart hangs out,' he explained, in deference to her lack of medical knowledge. 'What you're about to do is blow me to Glory!'

'I shall just have to take my chance on that.'

131

'Seems like it's me that's takin' the chance!'

'Very well; in that case I suggest you escort me back to Tombstone at once.'

He sighed, deeply; for he had grown fond of the girl – and in other circumstances, would have preferred not to kill her. Ah well, we can't always do as we'd like in this world, that's for sure.

'Maybe I'd better, at that,' he lied, smoothly. 'You don't mind, do you, if I leave a note for Kate? Her bein' out an' about doin' the household shoppin' an' all, she might take it kind of personal if you an' me jest high-tail it out of here, without tellin' her goodbye. You know what she's like. She acts a mite suspicious on occasion . . .'

He placed the tray carefully on the table, and began to reach for the pen he kept in his Derringer pocket.

She forestalled him.

'There's no need for that,' snapped Dodo. 'I've already attended to the matter. I've written a letter, explaining what we are about.'

So what could he do? Except face the inevitable; always an unpleasant experience.

'Well, I surely hope you've explained real good! O.K. then – since you appear to have taken care of every goddam thing, we'd best vamoose before she gets back an' gives us the kind of argument I wouldn't by no means wish to be a party of. By God, little girl – first you clean me out at poker, an' then you get the drop on me! When we *do* get to Tombstone, I'm gonna be right glad to observe your disappearin' rear end!'

So Doc Holliday rode off to keep his date with Destiny, and such, spurred to this course by a gun in the lower vertebrae and held there as a reminder that Dodo was right behind him in the saddle, and in a mood to tolerate no nonsense.

While Destiny and such, for their part, contrived to arrange that as the ill-assorted pair left town, Steven and Johnny Ringo rode into it from the opposite direction.

Destiny is uncommonly good at things like that.

'What makes you think,' enquired Steven, 'that they'll be in *this* town? It doesn't look the kind of place anyone would choose to visit.'

'I don't *know*, boy, but I surely do figure so. On account it's the first bar-fall out o' Tombstone, an' Doc'll be thirsty.'

'All right then – so, *if* they're here, how do we find them?'

'The way it mostly happens,' explained Ringo, 'is, *you* take one side of the street, while I take the other. And then,' he continued, 'what J. Caesar would have done, is try every saloon.'

'And if I find him first, how will I know him?'

'You'll know him, boy – you'll know him! An' if so be you do find him, don't try nothin' on your own. Holler fer me!'

'I'll be glad to,' agreed Steven, setting off on a tour of the unsavoury tourist traps and leaving Johnny to tie down his holsters, check his firing pins, and generally follow the accepted guide-lines laid down for gun-fighters, at such moments in their lives.

However, since we know that Holliday was no longer in residence, the whole scene might be said to lack dramatic tension; were it not for the fact that in the very first bar Ringo entered, Kate Elder, who had finished her shopping, was trying to earn a lile blameless pin-money at the Faro table.

And that encounter led to tension enough for anybody in their right mind.

'Whoops!' said Kate, on meeting Ringo's ice-cold eyes.

'Now what kind of a remark is that?' he enquired. 'Ain't you pleased to see me?'

'When am I never?' she assured him. 'Jest a mite unexpected, that's all. Well now, Johnny, it's been nice meetin' you again, but I really must be leavin' now, on account of shoppin' an' such . . . Woman's work,' she improvised, 'is never done!'

'So don't do it,' he advised. 'You got no call to go no place, as I can see. 'Less, of course, you plan to travel feet first?'

'Why, Johnny, you wouldn't gun down no frail female, would you?'

'Generally speakin', it's no trouble. But cain't say as I recollect your bein' frail, Kate. More like a bob-cat in a hen-coop, as I remember,' he said, his mind drifting back to their previous close relationship. 'But right now, that don't make no never mind. Reason I've come a-callin' is so's I can offer you my congratulations on your forthcoming nuptials.'

'Oh, those?' She dismissed whatever *they* were, with an airy wave. 'Most folks has 'em.'

'Which are indeed widely spoken of,' he continued. 'So what I would also like to do at this time is offer those same good wishes to the degenerate bridegroom.'

'Oh, him? I'd let it ride, if I was you, Johnny – he wouldn't thank you.'

'Reckon I'll chance that, after I've come all this way, so specific. Take me to him!'

And since his sensitive fingers were, she noticed,

playing a devil's tattoo on both gun-butts, our home-spun Delilah led him at once to the one-night love-nest. There she found Dodo's note and reacted to it like a powder-keg to a fast fuse.

'Why, the innocent-lookin' little prairie-flower!' she spat – or words to that effect. 'She an' Doc has cleared out to New Mexico!'

No fool, Miss Dodo Dupont.

'Mean to say,' asked Ringo, anxious to get everything straight, 'he's jilted you in favour of Regret's bespoken?'

'Looks that way,' she sighed. 'Ain't life a livin', breathin' cactus in the cushion?'

He considered the judgement, and found it hasty.

'Don't know about that,' he comforted her. 'Look at it *this* way, instead: here was I, about to kiss you an' Doc off to Hades – him first, an' then you!' he elaborated. 'But now, here we both are – two young people with a life of broken promises stretchin' before us to wherever . . .

'Now, New Mexico's a ways; so I reckon Doc'll jest have to wait patient till I can attend to his requirements at some future date. Because, lookin' on the bright side now, I have been offered gainful employment by the Clantons – an' you know you always wanted me to work steady a day or two . . .'

'Not, for God's sake, with the Clantons! They ain't in your kind of class, Johnny!'

He admitted that, by all accounts, they weren't company such as a mangy dog would choose to dine alongside of. 'But you know how it is,' he told her, 'these days of the dyin' West, you take what you can get. Which is why,' he added, tactlessly, 'I'm takin' *you* back . . .'

So, being a girl who had always known which side her

135

bed was bartered, she settled for that. And having whistled up Steven, and offered him their condolences on the tragic outcome of his love life, they set out, in their turn, for Tombstone – where the vultures certainly were gathering some.

And Steven, not being entirely sure where New Mexico might be, followed along . . . although just what he was going to say to the Doctor, Heaven alone knew!

And, for the moment, it wasn't telling . . .

22

The Entry of the Gladiators

Back at the Clanton Ranch, the atmosphere, never of the best, was now redolent of yesterday's hog-wash, left to get on with it in an air-tight container; Phineas having arrived at the homestead just previous, bearing Wyatt's pressing come one – come all to a sun-up conference at the O.K. Corral.

'But we gotta settle it sometime, Pa,' Ike was saying, 'an', for God's sake, there's four of us, ain't there?'

'An' three of 'em's you boys,' agreed Pa, ever the realist, 'while them two survivin' Earps is not only fast an' accurate, but consider they got a grievance. Thanks, that is, to you two goin' off premature, an' ventilatin' their little brother! You know how folks feel about their brothers – you've told me yourselves.'

They thought about the late Reuben Clanton; and it crossed their minds – which didn't take long – that, in fact, they hadn't liked him much anyway. But still an' all, a man's gotta do et cetera; and no doubt the Earps felt the same. If the boys had been figuring shrewd, they might have thought of that sooner; but it was, of course, too late now.

'Well,' said Phineas, searching for a silver lining, 'at

least Masterson ain't gonna be with 'em. That means they're as far outside the law as we are.'

'What it means,' said Pa, 'is that, 'less we emerge victorious tomorrow, I ain't gonna make Mayor; an' you boys can likewise whistle for any hopes you had of makin' Town Clerk, Borough Surveyor, an' Dog Catcher – which had been my dearest wish! 'Sides of which, we'll be dead!'

The sun was going down now, for want of anything to detain it; and as it sank towards the cactus-packed scenic attractions, three long shadows fell across the floor; and lay there, commanding general interest. Well, one long shadow, and two medium-sized ones, actually.

Pa was the first to track the phenomenon to its source.

'Well, Glory be!' he exclaimed. 'Slit me, if it ain't Johnny Ringo! Now we've maybe got a chance!'

Phineas wasn't sure. His keen eye had perceived that the pianola dude and that hellion choir mistress were also along.

'Pa,' he complained, 'for pity's sake, we don't want no musical evening, do we? I mean, seein' as how it's maybe our last?'

Night in the gaol-house was an event not much enlivened by the brooding presence of two mourning Earps and a less than sanguine Doctor, trying to learn how not to shoot his own foot off with a twelve-bore.

'For the love of your Eternal Salvation, Doctor,' said Wyatt, 'you hold it this a-way – pointing at the forces of Beelzebub – not at the Powers of Light!'

'I appreciate that,' said the Doctor, 'it's just that if at any juncture I need to ask your advice, then the weapon will tend to turn with me. Look...' he illustrated. As one Earp, they all ducked.

'Seems to me,' advised Bat, 'that you boys should let the old guy stay right here. What I mean is, cain't you jest rely on the threat of his presence? That should do it, I'd say. He sure enough scares the hell outa me!'

'Don't give me no argument, Bat,' said Wyatt. 'Since you seen fit to get a rush of yellow-livered conscience to the bowels, I'm gonna need him out there – if only to draw their fire. Now then,' he continued, wearily, 'we'll take it from the top, one more time. You place the buck-shot in the blunt end – so; and then you point it *away* from you; with your finger on the trigger, here ... *that's* the trigger ... got it?'

Dawn in Tombstone, October 26, 1881, and all these things occurring:

Johnny Ringo, riding in alone; he generally rode alone, remember?

Followed, after some time, and at a very discreet distance – silhouetted against the sunrise – by Ike, Phineas, Billy, their Pa and the yellow hound-dog, which had come along for laughs. All in that order.

Doc Holliday, who, the night previous, had checked in to the Last Chance, rising to shave his immaculate jowls.

Dodo, snoring delicately in the next room.

Wyatt, Warren, and the Doctor, stepping out into the centre of Main Street, jaws set – in one case, as with the onset of tetanus – on their doom-laden way to the widely anticipated holocaust.

Kate saying to Steven that, if so be as Ringo got his, then she'd always admired the type of man who knew his way round a keyboard, so what the hell? Why didn't they ride in to watch the big event, while making plans for the future?

Steven going along with it for now; because, frankly, he couldn't think what else to do at this point.

And all over the landscape, little groups of outlaws, ne'er-do-wells, and bad-hats, galloping in to witness the grand finale. Becase word had got around; and if so be as the Clantons won, then the town would be wide open, wouldn't it? Sure it would! Sure!

So – got all that, have you? Because all these strangely compounded concomitants are the stuff of legend!

Fine. So here we go, friends: The Gunfight at the O.K. Corral!

23

Come Sun-Up...

Ringo, of course, was early; as he might have known he would be, if he hadn't been so all-fired anxious to snatch the star part. So there were now two courses open to him, he figured: he could stand there, exuding menace like Attila the Hun at a poll-booth; casting his long shadow in all directions, until such time as the supporting cast arrived to back him up – the disadvantage of this being that he would look a mite foolish if they didn't show; which he wouldn't by no means put past them, having had some opportunity the previous night to study their sterling worth: or else he could kill a little time over a breakfast bottle at the Last Chance; and return later, to make the delayed appearance which is not only dramatically effective, but sometimes gets an entrance round.

So he settled for the latter alternative as being better from every point of view; and following a circuitous route to avoid Main Street, which he fancied might well be busy at this hour, he presently fetched up at the long-bar; where he remembered, with sudden irritation, that he had lately shot the bar-keep.

So he served himself.

*   *   *

But Ringo had underestimated the Clantons who, true to the few words they knew, were now arriving at the preordained scene of combat, one by one and as silently as they could contrive.

Dismounting, they hitched their horses – who had been afraid something like this might happen – in positions chosen to provide suitable cover; and then withdrew for a council of war into the darkness of the livery stable; where a roll-call swiftly established that Ringo was not yet amongst them.

'Damn!' said Pa. 'There ain't no other corral in town, is there? I mean, you boys did tell him exactly how to find this place?'

'Drew him a map,' said Phineas, proudly, 'with little arrows an' such . . . in coloured inks . . .'

'Oh God!' groaned Pa. 'That's all we needed . . .'

And then, to complete their enjoyment, they saw the TARDIS.

Dodo awoke from a dream of missed trains and lost opportunities, said 'Oh – surely it can't be that time!' and rushed into her captive's bed-room, to see if he was stirring yet.

As we have seen, he was shaving; and, at her precipitous entrance, cut himself, painfully. He really was going to be glad to see the back of this one and said so . . .

'Then hurry up!' she advised him. 'The sooner you take me to the Doctor, the sooner you'll be rid of me. You really can't expect me to comb an unpleasant town like this, all on my own!'

'How many times do I have to tell you, little lady,' said Doc, 'he'll be with Wyatt? So he'll keep till we get there, I'd say. There ain't no hurry.'

Little did he know!

'What in hell *is* that contraption?' demanded Ike.

'Like nothin' *I* ever seen before,' admitted Phineas.

'That don't prove a thing,' said Billy, offensively. 'Half the time you ain't capable!'

'Phin,' said Pa, slowly, 'you say it was Wyatt suggested we meet up here?'

'Far as I recollect. I mean, it weren't my idea – that's for certain sure!'

They believed him.

'Then I tell you what it likely is,' deduced Pa. 'I'll bet you five to a horse-laugh, that treacherous, bible-quotin' bastard has filled this here large-size sarcophagus with dynamite – or some such unsporting substance – which he will presently proceed to blow! Boys, stand not upon the order of your going, but get the hell outa here!'

And they broke cover, like bankers from a busted cathouse!

Meanwhile down the centre of Main Street strode the gallant Doctor, supported left and right, with vice-like grips to the elbows, by Warren and Wyatt.

I'm sure you can easily imagine the nerve-scraping accompaniment which would have been playing, had there been a symphony orchestra available. Because you should also realise that, by now, all first-floor windows were packed to their sashes by the previously reported assortment of rough-necks, bad-lots, and *personae non gratae*, waiting to see which way the cookie crumbled

143

before joining in.

Frank and Jack McLowry were there, for a start; as were Curly Bill, and Florentino Cruz, to name but several anti-social elements. In fact, such a collection of fancy-dressed desperados had seldom been previously assembled at the same time and place in the whole history of carnage. They had long been looking forward to seeing the Earps get theirs – and it looked as if this was likely it!

So the dice were somewhat loaded; and Blind Justice, on her pedestal over the Court-house, trembled accordingly.

It was about now that Johnny Ringo discovered he had left his copy of *The Gallic Wars* back at the ranch; so seeking light literary distraction before battle, as had been Caesar's constant habit, he cast an idle eye over the hotel register. And, on seeing the previous night's entry, all thoughts of the O.K. Corral were swept into abeyance by the call of more urgent personal business. He mounted the stairs with the surprised look of a man born in the saddle, and sought the first-floor back.

The sign of the decayed tooth still swung, groaning in the wind, from the charred ruins of Holliday's business premises; and as it came to the Doctor's attention, so did the sequence of events which had led so remorselessly to his present predicament; and he erupted with spluttering indignation.

'There it is!' he snapped. 'That's the whole cause of the trouble!' And he pointed to it with his shot-gun.

'*What* is?' asked Wyatt and Warren, jumping like

jack-rabbits – for the nervous tension was considerable. And was infectious – causing the Doctor to jump in his turn; whereupon both barrels exploded.

The first shot caught Curly Bill in the diaphragm; and the second brought Frank McLowry drifting lead-like to the street before them, in a shower of broken glass; these events coinciding with the breaking from cover of the Clantons – who promptly revised their plans, and sought fresh hide-aways, from which to assess the situation.

'If I was you, friend,' said Wyatt, laconically as always, 'I'd reload right smart!'

'Reload?' said the Doctor. 'But, good heavens, I never intended . . .'

'Never mind what you intended,' said Warren. 'Seems like you just made a pre-emptive strike!'

And, carrying the appalled Doctor between them, the Earps sprang, with an interesting Catherine-wheel effect, into the dubious shelter of the horse-trough.

The sound of shots fired in anger was something which had surrounded Holliday from infancy, so he continued imperturbably to settle his cravat; but not having his background, Dodo squeaked, and spun towards the door which, she now realised, she had carelessly left open. And framed in it, like a picture of a mortician touting for trade, twin six-guns at the ready, stood Johnny Ringo.

'Doc,' she gulped, 'I think you've got a smut on your nose . . .' And she held before his face a small hand mirror, such as young ladies carry at all times . . .

'Why, so I do declare!' said Doc. And he loosed an underarm shot behind him with his Derringer.

He had never previously attempted such a manoeuvre; but he had once seen Bill Cody perform this difficult feat to the detriment of Annie Oakley's hair-do, so he was interested to see the outcome, and was pleased to note that on this occasion it worked, the bullet taking the astonished gun-man in the place it would do most damage – no need to specify.

'Sorry, old friend and colleague,' said Holliday, sadly – for he'd always had a professional admiration for the man – 'but how you have the gall to come bustin' in here while I'm dressin' . . .'

'My gall,' said Johnny Ringo, a scholar to the last, 'is now divided into three parts . . .' And thereupon he quietly died, not, perhaps, *quite* like a gentleman, but going on that way.

'Little lady,' said Doc, mopping his face with the crêpe-edged bandana he kept for such occasions, 'I am surely obliged! And now let us see what is portended by the noise of the multitude . . . Only, if I was you,' he added, 'I would stay right where you are, until I have investigated same . . .'

And he sauntered forth, to see if he could be of any assistance to anyone.

'Well, Glory be!' smiled Wyatt, as his friend's dapper figure manifested itself on the sidewalk. 'We got company!'

'Confound the man!' objected the Doctor. 'He is the cause of this whole intolerable imbroglio!' And he inadvertently sent another shot in the approximate direction of the reinforcements.

'Maybe,' agreed Wyatt, 'but it would pleasure me some if you'd stop doing that! Over here, Doc . . .' he called.

Doc knew perfectly well where they were, but preferred to stay where *he* was – behind a newly perforated trash-can, in point of fact – till he had weighed all the relevant circumstances.

'What you plannin' to do, Wyatt?' he asked. 'Cain't jest lay there all the cock-eyed morning...'

'Gonna work round behind 'em,' explained Wyatt.

Doc groaned to himself. His friend, he sometimes felt, was sound, but limited...

'Seems to me,' he said, 'as they look pretty much the same, whichever side you see 'em. Come on now – you got Warren there, ain't you? Reckon the three of us can take 'em, face to face, like always.'

About to make good this confident claim by stepping into mid-thoroughfare, he paused briefly to suggest that maybe one of them might explain to that trigger-happy old buzzard that he, Holliday, was one of the good guys, and nobody's turkey at a Thanksgiving Shoot...

And this point having been established to his satisfaction, he strolled jauntily across the street to join them.

Surveying the scene from his temporary field-headquarters, back of the wooden Indian by the cigar store, Pa Clanton was chagrined to observe that the Earps were now supported by, not one, but a pair of doctorates – something which is always impressive...

'Hey, that ain't fair!' he hollered. 'They got *two* Hollidays with 'em!'

'Yeah – I meant to tell you about that...' said the ineffable Phineas.

The others just looked at him the way they did so

147

often. Ah, well . . .

'What do I do now?' asked the Doctor, after Holliday had enquired politely as to the current condition of his jaw. 'I mean, surely you don't need *me* any more?'

'Don't know about that,' said Wyatt. 'So far, you're doin' jest fine. So, reckon we'll keep you with us, for luck. An' since all innocent parties are now here assembled, kindly consider yourself free to shoot the first thing that moves!'

In fact, the Doctor was beginning to enjoy himself, rather; but unfortunately, the first thing that *did* move was Eddie Foy who had thought to improve the shining morning by passing out a few handbills. He now decided, as he retrieved his shredded head-gear, that if they thought the show was *that* bad, why then, a mid-week closing was not altogether unprecedented: and the disenchanted actor legged it for the stage-stop. They lamped his dampened flamboyance with passing interest.

'Who in hell was that?' asked Warren, bringing down Florentino Cruz with a casual left and right.

'Nobody special,' they assured him.

Ah! The transitoriness of theatrical fame!

And the boys in the gallery, reckoning they could tell well enough by now how this thing was going to turn out, left Frank, Curly and Florentino to make their own arrangements, and withdrew to Ma Golightly's.

Witnessing the departure of these unreliable floating voters, Pa thought, Hell, they might as well get it over.

So, lining up as if for a square dance, the Clantons and

148

the Earp faction advanced slowly towards each other along the shopping precinct.

Strictly speaking, no further dialogue was called for at this late stage in the proceedings, the parties involved being well aware of the formalities about to ensue. But blabber-mouth Billy, the fastest streak of lightning as ever called for a competent conductor, couldn't leave well alone, could he?

'Earp,' he called, 'I already sent your little brother to a high time in Hades! Time for you to join the action there, I'd say – '

Which was the last thing he *did* say; because shortly thereafter he had no further engagements to speak of on account of Wyatt and Warren, indulging in a certain amount of overkill, simultaneously shooting him in his rotten heart.

However, Doc Holliday, with untypical lack of judgement, chose to shoot Phineas in the head – wherefrom the flattened bullet ricochetted elsewhere with a petulant whine. So Phineas merely slept once more, another crease in his long-suffering skull.

And Pa himself was presently put out of action by the attachment of his faithful dog to an ankle of which it had happy memories.

Which left Ike; who was about to redress the balance of the casualty figures somewhat by drilling the Doctor, a thing to which he had been looking forward, when from behind him . . .

'Hands up!' said Steven Regret and Kate Elder, in their customary close harmony . . .

And Dodo came running from one end of the street, saying, so that's where they'd all been, while she'd been so anxious; and Kate from the other, saying as she'd always been faithful, and how could anybody ever have thought different?

And Doc raised an eyebrow, and left it at that for the time being.

So all friends were safely re-united at last – and fortunate to be so, in the unlikely circumstances.

On the side of the angels, Warren had acquired a bullet in the shoulder, and Doc a thirst – which was nothing unusual for either of them.

And Bat Masterson emerged cautiously from his gaol-house, noted the high proportion of corpses disfiguring the amenities of a town he was trying to keep clean – for God's sake! – and thought he'd better take some kind of positive action.

So he arrested Eddie Foy for causing an obstruction. And that was about it, really ...

'There's just one thing,' mused Wyatt, some time later in the O.K. Corral. 'Seems like only the other day, Doctor whatever your name is, you told me you was a master of legerdemain and prestidigitation? Whereas your recent performance on the shooting-iron does not incline me to support that vainglorious claim! Have you, by any chance, been guilty of providing me with false information, such as would be an offence unto the Lord?'

'Not at all,' said the Doctor. 'Now, if you'll all stand in a semi-circle, and stay quite still, my friends and I will show you a very difficult trick ...'

And they stepped into the TARDIS ...

Epilogue

'Well, of course,' said Doc Holliday, 'seein' as I'd been told about the surprisin' habits of that there infernal contraption by young Miss Dodo during the course of our sojourning together, personally I was not surprised any more than somewhat when it took off for points invisible.

'But Wyatt now, an' the others, they was struck a touch transmogrified themselves by the whole unprecedented event, an' you can't rightly blame them: which likely explains why nobody's ever seen fit to mention the occurrence previous to this day.

'I mean, a man don't want to be accused of intemperate hallucinations, when he's a Bible-quotin' officer of the law; and, as for Ike an' his Pa ... well, I suppose they was by nature so accustomed to such alcoholic unreliability of the eyeball, that they never said nothin', neither.

'As I recall, Wyatt made some crack about Elijah – who, I gather, was a well-known sky-chariot operator at one time; an' that was the end of it.

'But, as for me: I tell you, friend, that in a life devoted to the pursuit of violent an' bloody incident, I have never had me such a pleasurable rush of superfluous adrenalin to the nerve-endings as in those few, hell-poppin' days back there . . .

'Which is why,' he concluded, grinning all over his raddled and disreputable features, 'I have surely enjoyed rememberin' it all now . . .'

At this point in his extraordinary story, he lay back on his pillow; and I figured he was about ready to file his claim on Eternity.

Maybe he was at that; but suddenly he opened one bright eye, which encountered a previously unmolested bottle of the right stuff I had been foolishly hoping to save for the journey home.

'Pity to leave that,' he sighed; and – if you'll believe me – he knocked it back in three!

And *then* he died.

And I can't say I'm the least bit surprised.

DOCTOR WHO

0426114558	TERRANCE DICKS **Doctor Who and The Abominable Snowmen**	**£1.35**
0426200373	**Doctor Who and The Android Invasion**	**£1.25**
0426201086	**Doctor Who and The Androids of Tara**	**£1.35**
0426116313	IAN MARTER **Doctor Who and The Ark in Space**	**£1.35**
0426201043	TERRANCE DICKS **Doctor Who and The Armageddon Factor**	**£1.50**
0426112954	**Doctor Who and The Auton Invasion**	**£1.50**
0426116747	**Doctor Who and The Brain of Morbius**	**£1.35**
0426110250	**Doctor Who and The Carnival of Monsters**	**£1.35**
042611471X	MALCOLM HULKE **Doctor Who and The Cave Monsters**	**£1.50**
0426117034	TERRANCE DICKS **Doctor Who and The Claws of Axos**	**£1.35**
042620123X	DAVID FISHER **Doctor Who and The Creature from the Pit**	**£1.35**
0426113160	DAVID WHITAKER **Doctor Who and The Crusaders**	**£1.50**
0426200616	BRIAN HAYLES **Doctor Who and The Curse of Peladon**	**£1.50**
0426114639	GERRY DAVIS **Doctor Who and The Cybermen**	**£1.50**
0426113322	BARRY LETTS **Doctor Who and The Daemons**	**£1.50**

Prices are subject to alteration

DOCTOR WHO

	DAVID WHITAKER	
0426101103	**Doctor Who and The Daleks**	£1.50
	TERRANCE DICKS	
042611244X	**Doctor Who and The Dalek Invasion of Earth**	£1.50
0426103807	**Doctor Who and The Day of the Daleks**	£1.35
042620042X	**Doctor Who – Death to the Daleks**	£1.35
0426119657	**Doctor Who and The Deadly Assassin**	£1.50
0426200969	**Doctor Who and The Destiny of the Daleks**	£1.35
	MALCOLM HULKE	
0426108744	**Doctor Who and The Dinosaur Invasion**	£1.35
0426103726	**Doctor Who and The Doomsday Weapon**	£1.50
	IAN MARTER	
0426201464	**Doctor Who and The Enemy of the World**	£1.50
	TERRANCE DICKS	
0426200063	**Doctor Who and The Face of Evil**	£1.50
	ANDREW SMITH	
0426201507	**Doctor Who – Full Circle**	£1.50
	TERRANCE DICKS	
0426112601	**Doctor Who and The Genesis of the Daleks**	£1.35
0426112792	**Doctor Who and The Giant Robot**	£1.35
	MALCOLM HULKE	
0426115430	**Doctor Who and The Green Death**	£1.35

Prices are subject to alteration

DOCTOR WHO

0426200330	TERRANCE DICKS **Doctor Who and The Hand of Fear**	£1.35
0426201310	**Doctor Who and The Horns of Nimon**	£1.35
0426200098	**Doctor Who and The Horror of Fang Rock**	£1.35
0426108663	BRIAN HAYLES **Doctor Who and The Ice Warriors**	£1.35
0426200772	**Doctor Who and The Image of the Fendahl**	£1.35
0426200934	TERRANCE DICKS **Doctor Who and The Invasion of Time**	£1.35
0426200543	**Doctor Who and The Invisible Enemy**	£1.35
0426201485	**Doctor Who and The Keeper of Traken**	£1.35
0426201256	PHILIP HINCHCLIFFE **Doctor Who and The Keys of Marinus**	£1.35
0426201477	DAVID FISHER **Doctor Who and The Leisure Hive**	£1.35
0426110412	TERRANCE DICKS **Doctor Who and The Loch Ness Monster**	£1.25
0426201493	CHRISTOPHER H BIDMEAD **Doctor Who – Logopolis**	£1.35
0426118936	PHILIP HINCHCLIFFE **Doctor Who and The Masque of Mandragora**	£1.25
0426201329	TERRANCE DICKS **Doctor Who and The Monster of Peladon**	£1.35

Prices are subject to alteration

DOCTOR WHO

0426116909	Doctor Who and The Mutants	£1.35
0426201302	Doctor Who and The Nightmare of Eden	£1.35
0426112520	Doctor Who and The Planet of the Daleks	£1.35
0426116828	Doctor Who and The Planet of Evil	£1.35
0426106555	Doctor Who and The Planet of the Spiders	£1.35
0426201019	Doctor Who and The Power of Kroll	£1.50
0426116666	Doctor Who and The Pyramids of Mars	£1.35
042610997X	Doctor Who and The Revenge of the Cybermen	£1.35
0426200926	IAN MARTER Doctor Who and The Ribos Operation	£1.50
0426200616	TERRANCE DICKS Doctor Who and The Robots of Death	£1.35
042611308X	MALCOLM HULKE Doctor Who and The Sea Devils	£1.35
0426116586	PHILIP HINCHCLIFFE Doctor Who and The Seeds of Doom	£1.35
0426200497	IAN MARTER Doctor Who and The Sontaran Experiment	£1.35
0426110331	MALCOLM HULKE Doctor Who and The Space War	£1.35
0426201337	TERRANCE DICKS Doctor Who and The State of Decay	£1.35

Prices are subject to alteration

DOCTOR WHO

	0426200993	Doctor Who and The **Stones of Blood**	£1.35
	0426200594	Doctor Who and The **Sunmakers**	£1.50
☐	0426119738	Doctor Who and The **Talons of Weng Chiang**	£1.35
	0426110684	GERRY DAVIS Doctor Who and The **Tenth Planet**	£1.35
	0426115007	TERRANCE DICKS Doctor Who and The **Terror of the Autons**	£1.35
	0426115783	Doctor Who – The **Three Doctors**	£1.50
	0426200233	Doctor Who and The **Time Warriors**	£1.50
	0426110765	GERRY DAVIS Doctor Who and The **Tomb of the Cybermen**	£1.35
	0426200683	TERRANCE DICKS **Doctor Who and The Underworld**	£1.35
	0426201442	Doctor Who and An **Unearthly Child**	£1.35
	0426201353	ERIC SAWARD **Doctor Who and The Visitation**	£1.35
	0426200829	MALCOLM HULKE Doctor Who and The **War Games**	£1.50
	0426201469	JOHN LYDECKER **Doctor Who and Warriors' Gate**	£1.35
	0426110846	TERRANCE DICKS Doctor Who and The **Web of Fear**	£1.35
	0426113241	BILL STRUTTON **Doctor Who and The Zarbi**	£1.50

Prices are subject to alteration

DOCTOR WHO

0426192974	PETER GRIMWADE **Doctor Who – Time-Flight**	£1.50
0426201361	TERRANCE DICKS **Doctor Who – Meglos**	£1.35
0426193261	CHRISTOPHER H. BIDMEAD **Doctor Who – Castrovalva**	£1.50
0426193342	TERRANCE DICKS **Doctor Who – Four to Doomsday**	£1.35
0426193776	IAN MARTER **Doctor Who – Earthshock**	£1.35
0426193857	JOHN LYDECKER **Doctor Who – Terminus**	£1.50
0426193423	TERRANCE DICKS **Doctor Who – Arc of Infinity**	£1.35
0426195108	**Doctor Who – The Five Doctors**	£1.50
0426193938	PETER GRIMWADE **Doctor Who – Mawdryn Undead**	£1.35
0426194578	TERRANCE DICKS **Doctor Who – Snakedance**	£1.35
0426195299	**Doctor Who – Kinda**	£1.35
042619537X	BARBARA CLEGG **Doctor Who – Enlightenment**	£1.50
0426195531	IAN MARTER **Doctor Who – The Dominators**	£1.50
0426195612	TERRANCE DICKS **Doctor Who – Warriors of the Deep**	£1.50
0426195884	JOHN LUCAROTTI **Doctor Who – The Aztecs**	£1.50
0426196171	TERRANCE DICKS **Doctor Who – Inferno**	£1.50
0426196767	GERRY DAVIS **Doctor Who – The Highlanders**	£1.50
0426197801	CHRISTOPHER H. BIDMEAD **Doctor Who – Frontios**	£1.50

Prices are subject to alteration

THIS OFFER EXCLUSIVE TO

READERS

Pin up magnificent full colour posters of DOCTOR WHO

Just send £2.50 for the first poster and £1.25 for each additional poster

TO: PUBLICITY DEPARTMENT *
   W. H. ALLEN & CO PLC
   44 HILL STREET
   LONDON W1X 8LB

Cheques, Postal Orders made payable to WH Allen PLC

POSTER 1 ☐   POSTER 2 ☐   POSTER 3 ☐
POSTER 4 ☐   POSTER 5 ☐

Please allow 28 DAYS for delivery.

I enclose £ _____

CHEQUE NO. _____

ACCESS, VISA CARD NO. _____

Name _____

Address _____

_____

---

*For Australia, New Zealand, USA and Canada apply to distributors
listed on back cover for details and local price list